Peril in Paradise

Doug Fletcher Book 13
Dean L. Hovey

Print ISBNs

Amazon Print 9780228625698
BWL Print 9780228625681
Ingram Spark 9780228625704
Barnes & Noble 9780228625643

BWL Publishing Inc.

*Books we love to write ...
Authors around the world.*

http://bwlpublishing.ca

Acknowledgements

I owe much to my legion of subject matter experts, beta readers, proofreaders, an editor, a cover designer, and my publisher who all collaborate with me to make these books a reality. Julie puts up with my hours on the computer and my distant stare as the characters reveal themselves and the plot to me. Deanna Wilson dove into the expanded role of early proofreader, often reading and critiquing a few out of context pages at a time to correct the punctuation and suggesting a key character. Fran Brozo, Mike Westfall, Clem MacIlravie, and Brian Johnson offer plot critique and are my muses when I've written myself into a corner. Anne Flagge and Natalie Lund proofread and correct my typos and grammatical errors. Jude Pittman, of BWL Publishing, has been marvelously supportive in getting my books into the hands of my readers. Most of all, thanks to you, the readers who provide me with feedback, plot ideas, and the energy to write.

Dedication

To Larry and Betty Hawes

Table of Contents

*"Laze — a combination of the
words lava and haze — is the
product of a chemical reaction that
happens when 2,140° lava hits the
ocean. The sea water gets boiled,
creating a messy mix of
hydrochloric acid, steam, and tiny
glass particles. The noxious
plumes of laze…can cause lung
damage, eye and skin irritation,
and even death…"*

-Hawaii's Civil Defense

Chapter 1

"Go closer to the steam. I can get a shot of the hot lava hitting the water with the steam rising toward the moon."

"You're crazy, man. The wind is shifting, and the volcanic laze is drifting this way."

After unsuccessfully trying to twist in his seat to take a picture over his shoulder, the photographer unbuckled his seatbelt and leaned toward the helicopter's open door. Framing his picture through the camera's viewfinder he said, "Just one more shot, fifty feet lower and a hundred yards closer to the ocean."

The pilot hesitated and said, "Are you crazy?"

"C'mon, man. A shot with the lava flowing into the ocean and the full moon above the steam cloud will be a magazine cover."

"My license is already in jeopardy for flying here. I can't go any lower or closer to the steam."

Continuing to snap photos, the male passenger said, "The pictures I took last month could end your flying career…if they got out. Get me closer!"

"You said you'd destroyed those pictures," the pilot said over the intercom.

Before the photographer responded a gust of Kona wind buffeted the helicopter forcing the pilot to compensate with a violent jerk. Seated behind the pilot, the female passenger shrieked. "You idiot! Jocko fell out of the door!"

Checking the altimeter, the pilot drew a breath. "Jocko's fall from this altitude isn't survivable. We're going back."

"No!" the woman shouted into the intercom. Unbuckling her own seatbelt, she crawled on hands and knees to the open door. Hanging onto a seatbelt with one hand and the door's frame with the other, she searched the surface of the black lava for the photographer. The helicopter's downwash blew her hair wildly. "Land this thing, dammit! He'll need first aid."

Continuing to hover, the pilot uttered, "He'll need a mortician more than he needs first aid."

"Take us down. Now!"

Turning the helicopter toward the ocean, the plume of steam rose before them, a giant white cloud backlit by the full moon. "The wind is blowing the laze toward us. We have to go. Now!"

"We've got to pick up Jocko. Set this thing down!"

Glancing at the woman who was unstrapped and leaning out the door, the pilot knew an argument would be futile. The alternative, flying into the cloud of acid volcanic laze to pick up the injured, or dead, photographer, would be suicide. "No. We're returning to the heliport."

The woman turned her head and glared at the pilot. "If you don't land and save him, I'll report you to the FAA and you'll never fly again."

The cloud of volcanic laze billowed toward them, leaving no option except a quick turn toward the hills and a fast retreat. With adrenaline coursing through his system, the pilot started a gentle turn away from the ocean.

"No! You can't leave him! Land now or I'll have your license pulled and…"

Before the woman finished her threat, the pilot yanked the controls, tipping the helicopter on its right side, then banking hard to the left. He chose not to look back, envisioning the woman grabbing for something solid as gravity and momentum pulled her out of the open door.

Chapter 2

My ongoing search for National Park Service cold cases yielded a list of a dozen disappearances and unsolved assaults that piqued my interest. Reading through the scant and often personalized accounts of the events, I was disappointed by the rangers who'd written reports including nothing more than their incomplete impressions of the crime scenes. Having been a St. Paul cop and detective before becoming a Park Service investigator, I knew how important it was to state observations succinctly, without injecting bias into the report. It was apparent that most of them hadn't been cross examined on the witness stand where they had to defend their statements to a skilled defense attorney.

I was contemplating the reported disappearance of a Glacier National Park camper when my cell phone buzzed. "Fletcher," I said without looking at the caller ID.

"Hi, Doug. You and Jill just won an all-expense paid trip to Hawaii."

Unaccustomed to my new boss' voice, I quickly checked the caller ID which indicated that the call was from Jack Pardee. "What's going on in Hawaii, Jack?"

"A ranger in Volcanoes National Park discovered the bodies of two hikers. Apparently, they'd wandered into a restricted area and died there."

Thinking that a walk in Hawaii wouldn't usually result in a person's natural death, much less the death of two hikers, I asked, "What was their cause of death?"

"The report is in the database."

Logging into the NPS incident reporting system, I found the ranger's notes. "I'm looking at the report. It sounds like they wandered away from the trail after the gate was closed. I assume they were found a long way from the normal trails."

Jack sighed. "They were only about a hundred yards from the main trail across a lava flow. No explanation was given for their bodies being overlooked by the park's rangers and visitors for what appears to be several days."

"Not that a trip to Hawaii would be unpleasant. I'm wondering why the local rangers and police aren't investigating."

"It's complicated, Doug."

"Of course, it is. Otherwise, you wouldn't be offering to fly us from Texas to Hawaii."

"The assigned law enforcement ranger works as a part-time cop for the county of Hawaii. His report states that the cause of death was inhalation of volcanic gas."

"That seems reasonable."

"Doug, he wrote the report and closed the incident the same day the bodies were found. That was before he had the autopsy results. He's either really good, or he's an idiot who jumps to conclusions."

I sighed. "I've worked with a couple of cops who rushed to close cases. In that instance, it was because they were overwhelmed and were eager to close what appeared to be obvious cases."

"I'd like to believe that the responding ranger was seasoned and closed the case because the cause of death was obvious."

"You're talking about spending a lot of your budget to send Jill and me to Hawaii because you're not comfortable with the resident ranger's investigation. He could be spot on."

"I talked to Steve Langevin, the investigating ranger, yesterday. He's closed the case and isn't looking back."

I reread Langevin's brief report. "He might be one of those people who made up his mind and doesn't want to be bothered by the facts. You can request that the local police investigate."

"Langevin is also a part-time local cop, and maybe a good old boy. Hawaii County has also closed their investigation."

"There must be an FBI office in Honolulu that can send an agent to investigate."

"I spoke with the special agent in charge of the Honolulu FBI office. They've got everyone tied up in a human trafficking investigation and he's not willing to pull someone off to investigate a couple of hikers who died after wandering off the trail."

Turning away from the computer, I leaned back and stared at the ceiling. "Jack, my experience of jumping into jurisdictional disputes with close-minded locals hasn't been pleasant."

"That's why I want you and Jill to step into this. My sense is that Jill could charm the skin off a snake."

I tried to guess how Jill would react to the assignment. We'd just moved into a new house and the boxes weren't even unpacked. "Snakes shed their skin naturally, Jack."

Pardee laughed. "You know what I mean. Jill missed her calling when she wasn't appointed the US ambassador to Canada or England."

I took a deep breath and blew it out. "I'll talk to her and get back to you."

"Doug, this is a plush assignment and you two are the perfect team for this investigation. It'll be a trip to paradise."

"Jack, you and I both know jurisdictional disputes are more like stepping into a cowpie than like taking a vacation. Like I said, let me discuss it with Jill."

Jack paused. "I've already booked your tickets for two weeks. Anything past the end of the investigation is paid leave that won't count against your vacation time."

Realizing that the polite phone call wasn't an offered assignment, but a polite order, I replied, "The last time we had that *vacation* arrangement, we got dragged into a second investigation that nearly got us killed."

"Hawaii is a peaceful place, Doug. Like I said, it's paradise."

"It's July, Jack. I doubt that Hawaii holds the same charm in July that it has in January."

"I heard the climate is the same year 'round."

I hung up the phone and thought, *Yeah. Right.*

Chapter 3

I found Jill, my wife and investigative partner, walking from the parking lot carrying a cardboard tray of Starbucks coffees. "Wow. I could use a Starbucks."

Holding the tray out of my reach, she kept walking. "I'm trying to charm the interpretive rangers into letting me join them in looking for the last groups of Kemp's ridley sea turtles coming in to lay their eggs."

"Jack called with an assignment."

Without losing a step Jill asked, "Where?"

"Hawaii," I replied as I followed.

Jill chuckled. "Hawaiian parks have their own resources. Jack wouldn't send us there."

"Jack isn't satisfied with the local ranger's assessment of an incident. He wants us to review the case. Jack threw in an offer that he'll let us stay for whatever time is left on our two-week assignment without it counting against our accrued vacation."

Reaching the break room, Jill paused. "When does he want us to leave?"

"We didn't discuss a specific day. The bodies were discovered two days ago, so I assume he wants us to leave before the trail goes cold." My phone buzzed and I saw an email from our boss with an attachment. "Jack sent something more."

"Crime scene pictures?"

I opened the email and the attachment. "We fly out of Corpus Christi tomorrow morning."

Matt Mattson's voice startled me. "Where are you flying tomorrow?"

"Hawaii. Two hikers died and it appears that the local ranger did an incomplete investigation."

"Wow. You just moved into your new house. Have you even unpacked the boxes yet?"

I looked at Jill who smiled, apparently under the impression I was kidding. She walked into the break room with the coffee, leaving me in the hallway with Matt. "The timing stinks but that's how investigations come up."

Matt shook his head. "Jill didn't believe you. Buy flowers."

"We're leaving tomorrow, Matt. The flowers will be dead by the time we return."

"You are so clueless. Buy them. Let Jill enjoy them tonight. Mandy will collect them after you leave and will replace them with fresh ones before you return."

I heard laughter inside the break room. Assuming that Jill had charmed the rangers into inviting her along to search for sea turtles, I handed Matt my VISA card.

"What's your price point?" he asked.

"Something less than redecorating the house."

"You might want to lower that ceiling a bit. Mandy likes to go big."

* * *

I spent the afternoon looking for information about Volcanoes National Park deaths, and specifically the most recent deaths of the two hikers. I was surprised that visitor deaths were relatively rare in the Hawaiian park, most resulting from falls, followed by heart attacks, and heat stoke. Having spent the afternoon in the July Texas sun, the inside of Jill's pickup was like an oven. We stood alongside the pickup with the doors open while we waited for the air conditioning to cool the seats. Jill had been quiet all afternoon, so I wondered where her head was in relation to the Hawaiian assignment.

"A penny for your thoughts."

"I'm getting excited about going to Hawaii, but I'm surprised Jack is sending us instead of using local resources."

"He asked for us specifically because of our skills. We're special. He values our unique skills, and he wants to tap into our expertise as a cop and former park superintendent." I paused, then added, "We should probably wear our uniforms there."

"I thought Hawaii was casual. You know, 'hang loose.' I plan to wear shorts and Hawaiian shirts."

"Bring your Florida swimsuit. We'll have time to visit a beach after we close the case."

"I'll buy a swimsuit there. Maybe I'll buy two. They dry so slowly in the tropical humidity. I'm sure the Hawaiian shops will have a great selection." I must've grimaced when recalling our Florida bathing suit shopping experience. Jill's eyes sparkled, realizing I'd left her an opening to needle me. "You'll be able to find something to do while I'm checking out the selection."

Reflecting on our Florida swimsuit shopping experience, I grimaced. Jill had difficulty finding a swimsuit to fit both her trim figure and her sense of modesty. As a woman in her fifties, she'd struggled to find a suit that ticked off both of those boxes. I'd spent more than an hour reading outdated magazines near the cash register while she'd tried on more than a dozen suits.

With the pickup's interior cooling, Jill stepped into the cab. "What did Jack tell you about the case?"

I spent the half-hour drive down the length of Mustang Island filling her in on the few details I'd received, and a subsequent review of the scant report filed by the investigating ranger.

It was strange driving to a house we owned instead of the townhouse we'd rented for over a year. Our new house was small, with an equally small yard that featured a well-kept flower garden. The previous owner had nursed the garden back to health after Hurricane Harvey had ripped Port Aransas to pieces. I unlocked the door and held it open for Jill. Focusing on returning my keys to my pocket, I was surprised to bump into Jill who'd abruptly stopped just inside the door.

"Did you spray deodorizer before we left?"

"No, why?"

She tipped her head back and inhaled. "Sniff."

The light scent of flowers filled the entryway. My discussion with Matt about flowers came to mind. "Check the dining room."

A large vase sat in the middle of the dining room table. Aside from some poppies, I didn't recognize most of the flowers, but the look on Jill's face told me she was pleased. She walked to the table and removed the small envelope tucked among some tall stalks covered with yellow flowers.

Biting her lip, Jill tapped the card on the table. "The note says they're from you, but the handwriting looks like Mandy's."

"It was a joint effort."

Setting the card aside, Jill wrapped her arms around my neck. "I'm sad that we can't stay here to enjoy the flowers and unpack."

"The boxes will be waiting for us when we get back. I should take cargo pants, so I'll open the ones we packed with clothes."

I was confused when Jill laughed. "Mandy and I are continuously updating *my* clothes. If God is giving anyone a sign, it's for you. When did you last buy a new pair of pants?"

"My old pants are comfortable."

"You've still got olive drab boxers from the Minnesota National Guard. How many decades old are they?"

"When I mustered out, they told us we were part of the inactive reserves and needed to have a uniform ready in case we're called up."

"Like you could fit into a uniform that you wore when you were nineteen. Hell, you can barely button the uniform pants you bought when we lived in Arizona." Anticipating my response, Jill shook her head. "No, those pants did NOT shrink in the dryer. All my uniforms fit just fine."

"All right. I'll find an outlet mall in Hawaii, and I'll buy a couple of shirts and some shorts."

"Cheapskate! We'll go into a real store where normal people shop, and you'll buy full price clothing that fit and are stylish."

"Men's clothing doesn't go out of style."

"Right. You didn't notice the eight-inch-wide paisley necktie I threw away when we moved to Texas."

"That was a classic!"

The smile left Jill's face and she put her head on my shoulder. "The boxes will still be sitting here when we return, and the flowers will be dead."

"I'm sure Mandy will take care of the flowers."

The doorbell interrupted our discussion. Matt was there holding a huge aluminum pan and Mandy was behind him with a six-pack of beer and a bottle of pre-mixed margaritas. "We brought supper."

Mandy pushed past me and herded Jill into the kitchen where they had a hushed conversation. "What's in the pan?" I asked.

"Smoked brisket, corn on the cob, cornbread, and beans. If you move that oversized garden off the dining room table, I'll set it down."

"Thanks for the flower suggestion."

Matt smiled as he returned my VISA card. "You made my wife happy. She loves spending other people's money."

Jill arrived with plates while Mandy took plastic margarita glasses out of the shopping bag. "What are the yellow stalks, Mandy? I've never seen a flower like them."

Mandy handed Jill a margarita. "They're foxtail lilies. Don't they look nice with the red poppies and bluebells?"

"They're lovely," Jill replied as she sipped her drink.

In a stage whisper, I spoke to Matt. "You'll notice that she didn't ask me what the yellow flowers were."

Mandy broke into laughter as she set paper plates on the table. "Men are so clueless when it comes to flowers. You would've bought roses."

"Roses are nice," I said as Matt opened the twist-top beer.

"Men buy roses because it's the only flower they recognize," Mandy explained as she peeled back the aluminum foil covering the food.

"I recognize carnations," I replied.

"Oh, Jill. This one's a keeper; he recognizes two varieties of flowers."

We laughed through supper and a second round of drinks. Mandy insisted on helping with the cleanup, then she and Jill packed items from the refrigerator that wouldn't be edible after our two weeks in Hawaii.

As they left with the perishable groceries, I hugged Mandy. "Thanks for buying the flowers."

She kissed my cheek. "You're welcome. I'm always available to spend your money."

Mandy gently pushed me away and hugged Jill while Matt shook my hand. "I hope the trip goes well."

"Investigations aren't good or bad, they're just a job."

"Try not to get shot."

"Why would I get shot investigating dead hikers?"

Matt shrugged, then asked rhetorically, "Why would you get shot looking for lost surveyors or trying to find a guy who dumped a body in an Arizona swamp?"

I cleared the table and took out the trash. With the doors locked, I took Jill's hand. "I'm sorry we're taking off for Hawaii with our new house still a mess."

"Like you said, we don't get to choose when assignments come up." She paused and smiled while looking at the flowers backlit by moonlight. "The flowers were a nice touch. Did you come up with that idea all by yourself or did Mandy suggest them?"

"Matt made the suggestion. Mandy executed the plan." I paused and looked at the piles of boxes. "Do you have any idea where my 'go bag' is?"

"It's with mine in the trunk of your car, dear. I anticipated a rapid departure for somewhere."

"You probably thought that trip would be to South Dakota after a call from one of our elderly parents."

Jill sighed. "We're at a point where any phone call could throw all our plans into disarray. If it hadn't been Jack's call, it would've been one of our mothers who needed us."

"Mandy's picking us up early," I said over my shoulder as I walked to the bedroom. "We should get some sleep."

Jill stepped in front of me as I surveyed the boxes and suitcases piled in the bedroom closet. She smiled as she unbuttoned my shirt. "We're going to spend a lot of hours on planes tomorrow. I'll sleep then."

"You know I can't sleep on a plane…"

Tugging out my shirttails, Jill smiled. "I guess you'll be tired when we land in Hilo."

I nuzzled Jill's neck. "I should buy flowers more often."

"You should."

Chapter 4

Being a small satellite airport, Corpus Christi flights connect through Houston or Dallas. From Houston, we caught a flight to LA where we had a three-hour layover while awaiting our flight to Hilo. We ate an expensive meal in a chain restaurant near our gate. Jill poked at the chicken in her taco salad.

"I keep forgetting that it's impossible to get real Mexican food when eating at a chain restaurant."

Setting aside my pulled pork sandwich, I nodded. "And California barbecue isn't like Rudy's."

That comment perked Jill up. "Remember when we went to Rudy's before we were married and the guy at the counter kidded you because you didn't know the difference between wet and dry smoked brisket?"

"Yeah, I think he was hitting on you."

"Nah, he was just having a good time kidding the Yankees who hadn't experienced Rudy's ambiance."

"I hope that we can find excellent seafood in Hawaii."

Pushing aside her half-finished meal, Jill looked toward our gate where a dozen people were lined up awaiting their turn to speak to the harried gate agent. "What are the chances we'll get upgraded to business class seats?"

"I expect we'll be in the sardine can seats the government travel agency booked for us. It looks like the plane will be full."

"Did you check your email this morning to see if there was any new information on the case?"

"Not before we left home," I replied. "Federal rules prohibit us from accessing email or secure Park Service websites from public WiFi."

A waiter appeared and dropped off a bill, then cleared our plates as Jill tapped information into her smartphone. Our meal cost as much as our weekly trip to the Port Aransas grocery store. I inserted my charge card into a small electronic box on the table and was amused that the options for payment included pre-calculated tip amounts ranging from ten to thirty percent. Considering that we'd placed our orders electronically, had our food delivered by someone from the kitchen, and had only seen our waiter when he delivered the bill, I chose the ten percent tip.

While I waited for the box to print the receipt, I commented, "This reminds me of using the self-checkout option at the grocery store."

Jill glanced up from her phone. "Just be glad they didn't expect us to prepare the meal ourselves."

"For nearly a hundred dollars, you'd think they'd at least refill our drinks." Jill's focus on her cell phone was annoying me. "Are you playing games or texting with my mother?"

After touching a few keys, she looked up. "The Park Service forbids using the unsecured airport WiFi, but I can access their database from the 5G internet from my phone." She handed me her phone. "I found the coroner's report on the Hawaii PD database."

"I think the point is to not open the NPS databases through unsecured WiFi. Using your phone is not…"

She cut off my lecture by saying, "I'm using 5G, which is not WiFi, and I'm not accessing any Park Service databases. Read the report."

As the investigating NPS ranger had noted in his report, the hikers had died from inhalation of toxic volcanic gas, causing their lungs to fill with liquid. The coroner noted the cause of death as suffocation due to hydrogen chloride induced pneumonia.

"I guess the ranger's first assessment was right on target." I held out the phone to Jill.

"Read on."

Jill's suggestion surprised me. Sensitive to the diners sitting near us, she'd seen something more that she couldn't discuss in a crowded restaurant. Further down the report, I found the coroner's general observations. "Although the bodies are badly decomposed, a closer analysis shows decomposition due to acidic gasses. The lack of cadaverine odor, indicative of enzymatic decomposition and bacterial attack, indicates that the bodies were found within 24 hours of death."

Carefully composing my response to Jill, I said, "The discovery was fresh."

She nodded. "The ranger didn't mention that assessment."

"The ranger may lack the expertise to make that analysis," I replied. "Most rangers aren't trained to make that kind of assessment."

"Read on."

Further down the report, the coroner added, "The femoral fractures with localized bleeding indicate trauma caused by a fall shortly before death."

I slid the phone back to Jill. "We need to speak with the report's author."

After exiting the database and shutting down her phone, Jill picked up her carry-on bag. "Let's find seats nearer the gate." As we exited the restaurant, she leaned close. "I don't understand the technical jargon, but I know that these weren't two people who wandered off the trail and were overcome by volcanic gas."

"Unless their bodies were found at the bottom of a cliff, something else was going on."

The gate agent paged, "Fletcher, party of two, please approach the desk."

As we approached, the gate agent stepped from behind the desk and met us. "Are you federal agents?"

Jill nodded.

"The gentleman in the blue blazer would like to speak with you." She nodded toward a man standing across the concourse from the gate. He smiled when we looked toward him.

"Why would he want to speak with us?" I asked the gate agent.

"You have the same employer," she said before returning to the desk.

We carried our bags across the concourse and set them near the smiling stocky, white-haired man.

"I'm Larry Hawes, your friendly air marshal. What are your names and which agency do you work for?"

"We're Doug and Jill Fletcher, from the National Park Service," I replied.

"I've never met an armed park ranger."

"We're with the Investigative Services Branch. All ISB employees carry firearms."

"I'm happy to have backup, but please try not to punch a hole through the fuselage if you feel compelled to discharge your firearms. A rapid decompression event makes a mess."

Jill smiled. "Thanks for your words of wisdom."

Nodding, Larry surveyed the crowd gathering near the boarding gate. "Get in line when they make the pre-boarding announcement. Put your carry-on bags overhead, take your seats, but don't buckle your seatbelts until they close the cabin door."

Jill and I both surveyed the passengers. "Is there a specific threat?"

"Not an overt threat, but I don't like the look of the college-aged kids who just came out of the bar. If I had to guess, they're probably already drunk and are going to order more alcohol on the plane. People like that tend to make the flight attendants' lives miserable."

Jill covered her mouth while appearing to scratch her nose. "We had an…experience with a businessman who'd been overserved on a flight."

I turned away from the crowd and adjusted the windbreaker that covered my badge and holster. "They're an annoyance. Is there anyone or anything here that scares you?"

Larry chuckled. "The risk level is orange, but realistically, I'm more concerned about catching Covid here in the lobby than I am about a terrorist or hijacker."

"That's nice, but not entirely reassuring," I replied.

"Hey, they still put air marshals on random flights just to keep an eye on things."

"Do you at least get to spend a few days on the beach before you fly back to the mainland?"

"First of all, there's no beach in Hilo. Secondly, I'll be in a *mauka*-view room in the cheapest Hilo hotel. Thirdly, after two nights of crappy sleep, I'll be on a red-eye flight to the mainland."

"What's *mauka*-view mean?" Jill asked.

"That's Hawaiian for mountain-view. All federal employees get *mauka*-view rooms. The tourists pay big bucks for the *makai*-view rooms, the ocean view." The gate agent made the pre-boarding announcement and Larry picked up his carry-on bag. "Like I said, try not to shoot a hole in the airplane."

Reaching down for her bag, Jill said, "I'll try, but we end up shooting someone on most every trip."

Larry snorted. "I've never met a federal cop who's discharged his weapon anywhere but on the firing range. It just doesn't happen." He walked to the lineup of handicapped travellers and people with children preparing to pre-board.

Jill looked at me. "You didn't tell him about our experiences?"

"Nah, he's better off not knowing."

* * *

Thankfully, the Hilo flight was uneventful. The college students were loud, but not obnoxious, and most of the passengers appeared to be looking forward to a vacation. There wasn't a Park Service ranger to greet us as we deplaned, nor was there an escort at the luggage carousel. Since all the midsize cars were out, the rental clerk upgraded us to a pickup which suited our taste better than the other option, which was a minivan.

After carefully using a yellow highlighter to show us the best route to the government's chosen hotel, the car rental woman looked at Jill. "Ma'am, I hope I'm not out of line, but I'd tell your boss that the motel lost your reservation, and I'd move to the Homestead B&B."

"Is there some reason we'd prefer the B&B to that motel?" Jill asked as I studied the map.

The young clerk wrinkled her nose. "You've heard that Hawaiian cockroaches are the size of pecans?"

Getting the hint, Jill took the map from me. "I think we got lost on our way to the motel. Highlight the route to the B&B you suggested."

The smiling clerk handed Jill a brochure for the B&B, then pulled out another map and highlighted a new route. "I think you'll like this better. There's nothing worse than having a two-inch cockroach flying into your mouth while you're asleep."

"They fly?" I asked.

"Oh, yes! And our ants are tiny specks that crawl everywhere."

Jill took the map. "Got it. Your cockroaches are big, and the ants are small. Is there anything else we should know about this slice of paradise?"

"The banana bread and Kona coffee are heavenly."

I tossed the keys to Jill as we walked to the only pickup in the parking lot. She clicked the remote, unlocking the truck. As I loaded our suitcases and carry-on bags into the back seat she said, "I doubt that the banana bread or Kona coffee are enough to overcome the taste of a cockroach in my mouth."

"Maybe the cockroaches are tangy or sweet," I said as I climbed into the passenger seat.

"Trust me. I've lived in enough seedy places across the South. Cockroaches have a distinctive, unpleasant odor. I assume they're like antelope, whose meat tastes the same as their smell."

"You've never mentioned eating antelope."

"That's because I didn't want you to think it was something I'd ever repeat. Antelope steak is right up there on the *never to be repeated list* alongside fried liver and Rocky Mountain oysters."

"You don't like your liver fried?"

That comment got a glare. "Smartass. I don't eat liver regardless of how it's prepared."

The Homestead B&B had a very small sign at the end of the driveway. After driving by it twice, Jill spotted it on the third pass. "Talk about understated advertising."

"You'd almost think they were trying to avoid business."

The driveway was two cars wide and barely longer than the pickup. Jill parked blocking a garage door. "I'll park on the street after we check in."

The door opened before we got to the steps, and a matronly Hawaiian woman with salt and pepper hair, and a broad smile greeted us. "*Aloha!*"

"I can move the pickup…"

The woman waved off Jill's comment. "That garage stall is just for the lawnmower. You're fine where you're parked."

The inside of the two-story house was filled with the scent of flowers and cinnamon. The living room furniture wasn't new but was well cared for. Magazines on the coffee table were current, with lovely cover pictures of waterfalls and flowers.

"I'm Mary Johnson, the owner, cook, and maid. If you need anything, you'll usually find me in the kitchen. If I'm not there, knock on the bedroom door under the stairs."

"I'm Doug Fletcher and this is my wife, Jill. I hadn't expected to meet any Johnsons in Hawaii."

Mary's smile widened. "I recognize your Minnesota accent. You come from the land of Johnsons and Carlsons."

"My Minnesota accent?"

Mary laughed. "I half expected you to say, 'you betcha,' or 'uff da.'"

"It's the darned *Fargo* movie. Everyone thinks Minnesotans talk like that."

"Doug, you've softened the accent a bit, but you still draw out the vowels when you speak. Where's home for you, Jill?"

"South Dakota."

Mary laughed. "I bet you met at a cross-border square dance."

Jill smiled. "We actually met during an Arizona murder investigation."

"I was going to ask about your pistols. You don't see anyone but cops carrying a gun around here…well, except for the pig hunters." Mary waved her hand. "Enough chit chat. You've been travelling all day. Let me show you to your room, and we can talk over breakfast. You're at the top of the stairs."

"Mary, don't we have to sign in and give you our credit card?" I asked.

Picking up the largest suitcase, Mary walked up the stairs while talking over her shoulder. "I don't expect that a couple Midwest cops will run out on me. We can deal with the bookkeeping after you're rested and fed."

"You act like you knew we were coming," Jill said as we followed our host.

"Ailani called from the car rental place. She said she'd steered you here instead of letting you go to the cockroach motel."

"The cockroach motel?" I asked.

"That's what we call the place where you were booked. She cancelled your reservation there."

"I suppose we'll be stuck with at least one night's charges," I said.

"I doubt it. They'll make more renting your room to someone else. The government rate barely covers the cost of laundering the sheets."

"Is that a problem here, or don't you accept government credit cards?" I asked as Mary opened our bedroom door.

"I'm a better negotiator than Havika. He's young and intimidated by the government travel people. I tell them I won't take a loss on their business and give them a fair price. They whine but accept my price in the end."

"Do you get a lot of government business?" Jill asked, looking at the large bedroom's sliding doors leading to a balcony overlooking the distant ocean.

"Quite a few government people move here after a night with Havika."

Jill laughed as she slid the balcony door open, allowing in the gentle plumeria-scented breeze. "They don't like cockroaches?"

"The roaches, the marijuana smoke, the loud music, and the traffic. This is much more peaceful than the motel." Mary gestured toward an open door. "That's your bathroom. All the personal care products are locally made with natural floral scents."

Jill elbowed me. "Gee, Doug. You'll smell like a flower garden instead of Old Spice."

"I don't use Old Spice..."

Mary held her knuckle under her nose, partially hiding her smile. "Ailani said she thought you two were married, but she wasn't sure. I won't need to roll in a cot for Doug to sleep on."

Jill sighed. "If he snores, you may find him sleeping on the living room couch."

"If I snore?"

Mary walked to the door. "Breakfast is served from six to eight o'clock. I'll take the banana bread out of the oven at six-thirty."

Chapter 5

Given the four-hour time difference between Texas and Hawaii, Jill and I were awake and showered well before the aroma of baking banana bread drifted into our room. Mary had just placed loaves on the cooling rack when we entered the small dining room off the kitchen.

"There's a coffee urn on the sideboard and hot water for tea in the white thermos. Are papayas okay with you, or would you prefer mangos?"

"Papayas are great," I replied as I drew coffee into mugs.

Half papayas were delivered as we sat. "The strawberry papayas at the farmer's market were very nice this week." After setting the papaya halves in front of us, Mary stepped back. "I can prepare eggs or Egg Beaters any way you'd like them. Or, I have tofu or cottage cheese. I also have bacon, turkey sausage, and ham."

I picked up a spoon and scooped out a piece of nicely ripe papaya. "I'd like a couple eggs, over easy, with a side of bacon."

Jill looked at the papaya, then at Mary. "A slice of your lovely banana bread will be plenty for me after eating this papaya."

From the kitchen, Mary spoke to us. "I didn't get a chance to ask what brought you to Hawaii."

Between spoonful's of papaya Jill replied. "We're here to investigate the death of the hikers in Volcanoes National Park."

"That's been in the paper. It's so sad, and it's bad for tourism."

"What's the unofficial view of the deaths?" I asked.

Mary sighed. "*Hoales* aren't smart about volcano risks. If not for the rangers, I swear that some ill-informed tourist would hike right into molten lava."

"*Hoales*?" I asked.

"That's what the local people call the tourists." Mary smiled. "We tell them it's a term of endearment."

"Rangers deal with clueless visitors all the time in the national parks," Jill replied. "People walk up to buffalos, alligators, and bears to take photos. We post signs all over warning visitors that the animals are wild and sometimes dangerous, but many seem to think they're visiting a petting zoo."

Mary returned with plates and set them down in front of us. Turning away, she drew a cup of coffee and sat next to Jill. "I hope you catch whoever did this."

Jill turned her head. "I thought the deaths were an accident?"

Mary wrapped her fingers around the coffee mug while she considered her response. "I have a cousin who works at the hospital where they did the autopsy. She said that hikers don't usually have broken legs from a walk across lava."

"We were told that they died from inhaling volcanic steam," I replied, trying to get Mary to open up without revealing that we knew anything beyond what was in the newspapers.

"I'm sure the laze killed them, but there's more."

"Laze?" Jill asked.

"It's the term for volcanic steam formed when the hot lava hits the ocean," Mary explained. "The laze plume is filled with droplets of hydrochloric acid and microscopic glass particles. Most of the time we have trade winds that blow the laze away from land, over the ocean. If we get a Kona wind, like we had last week, the Park Service closes the Chain of Craters Road and Hawaii Civil Defense issues advisories for people with lung problems to stay inside. By the time the laze blows this far inland, it's more irritating than dangerous. Nearer to the ocean, it's potent and deadly."

"Is that the rotten egg odor I smelled when I stepped onto the deck?"

"That's different. You're smelling sulfur dioxide vog — volcanic fog — created by the gasses escaping from the lava vents. It's annoying, but it won't kill you unless you walk right up to the source."

Jill nodded. "Laze is caused by the lava hitting the ocean and is deadly. Vog comes from lava vents and is stinky but not as dangerous. Good to know."

* * *

Armed with full bellies and Mary's local information, we drove south, looping around the southeastern portion of the island of Hawaii to the headquarters of Volcanoes National Park. The superintendent's office was located inside the Kilauea Visitor Center which overlooked a volcanic caldera. The odor of sulfur dioxide tickled my nose as I opened the pickup's door.

"Are we sure this is healthy?" I asked as we walked to the visitor center. I watched a small column of steam rise from the bottom of the caldera next to the parking lot.

"I'm sure they monitor the air quality," Jill said without hesitation. "As a superintendent, I used to get closure information from all the parks. This portion of the park was rarely closed, but the Chain of Craters Road, running past older lava flows, is closed any time the lava flows into the ocean and the wind shifts to the southeast."

Recalling our discussion with Mary I said, "Got it. The Park Service closes the roads when the Kona winds blow toward the island, instead of the prevailing trade winds that carry the volcano gasses over the ocean."

Joining a group of visitors inside the building, we wandered past historical information about formation of the Hawaiian Islands, the more recent lava flows, and an exhibit explaining why Hawaiian lava flows in rivers in contrast to Mount St. Helens' lava that caused an explosive eruption.

I stopped in front of a glass case displaying a burned boot. Reading the information, I learned about another ranger hazard beyond lightning strikes, charging bears, and venomous snakes. "The ranger wearing this boot broke through the crust over a lava flow and stepped down into molten lava."

Being a stoic realist, Jill considered my words for a second then said, "I'm surprised there was anything left of the boot. The lava is about 1,200° Celsius." She urged me ahead.

"I wonder what that is in Fahrenheit?" I asked, trying to remember the conversion factor I hadn't used since a high school chemistry class.

"Do you really think that matters when you break through the crust? Think of the lava running into the ocean. The heat is so intense that the water vaporizes before they actually touch. The visitor center probably has video showing the vaporizing steam blowing molten lava bits into the air."

At our request, a smiling volunteer directed us to the park superintendent's office. I waited for Mike Patton to finish his call before knocking on the door. He turned, smiling. "Can I help you?" His wavy white hair and tanned face had a movie star look. His cleft chin reminded me of an older version of the movie star Robert Mitchum.

I led Jill into the superintendent's office and offered my hand. "I'm Doug Fletcher. This is my partner, Jill."

Patton looked somewhat confused. "It's nice to meet you. Did we have a meeting?" He glanced at the badges on our belts and our sidearms.

"We're the National Park Service investigators from Texas."

"Ah," he replied as his smile melted away. "I'm afraid you've wasted your time."

"May we sit?" I asked.

Patton gestured to the guest chairs across from his desk. "Certainly. I thought you'd probably heard that the hiker's deaths were an accident. The case has been closed."

Jill leaned forward, trying to appear non-threatening. "We were asked to investigate. Even if the deaths were an accident, the Park Service would like to establish the cause and circumstances of the deaths so a corrective action plan can be put in place."

Patton stood, then walked to the door and closed it. "We have safeguards in place," he said as he returned to his desk. Pointing to a map of the park, he indicated the southern edge. "There are usually trade winds that blow the plume of volcanic steam and laze away from the park. We monitor the wind direction and weather forecast carefully. There are windsocks here at the visitor center and also on the lava flow. If the usual north-westerly trade winds change, a southeasterly Kona wind blows the laze cloud over the lava flow. When that happens, we close the Chain of Craters Road. There are times when we've also closed this visitor center when there's a significant vog cloud coming out of the crater with a Kona wind blowing toward the building. Other times we've closed the loop road around the visitor center if there's a significant vog cloud and trade winds."

Patton's lecture showed an irritating condescension, as if he were speaking to grade school children. I attempted to remain professional. "According to your ranger's report, even with all those safeguards, two hikers got onto the lava flow and were overcome by volcanic laze."

"The Chain of Craters Road was closed," Patton replied. "We can't control stupidity."

Jill was about to reply, but I put my hand on her arm, letting the silence make Patton uncomfortable.

After waiting a beat, Patton said, "It's just like the visitors who fall over the rim at the Grand Canyon. Stupid people climb over the railings to take selfies. It's not the park's fault if they fall."

Jill nodded. "Every death is a stain on the park's reputation. Every death should be followed by an investigation that identifies the root cause and suggests remedies to prevent a recurrence. We didn't see any root cause analysis or remediation plan in your ranger's report."

"Steve, our law enforcement ranger, did an investigation." Patton stood and pointed to the park map mounted on the wall alongside his desk. Placing his finger on a spot where three roads intersected, he said, "Steve attributed the deaths to hikers bypassing the closure gate, here. From there, they walked down the Chain of Craters Road to the lava flow, here."

I stood and walked across the office to the map. Looking at the map's scale, in the bottom corner, I used my fingers to estimate a one-mile distance, then measured off the Chain of Craters Road.

"That's quite a hike. It looks like it's about twenty miles."

Patton frowned. "The road is nineteen miles long."

Jill sensed my frustration with Patton and stepped in before I said something inappropriate. "Experienced hikers only move two to three miles an hour. It would've taken them more than six hours to trek down to the lava flow, assuming they didn't make any sightseeing stops along the way."

Patton looked annoyed. "Yes. That's what hikers do. They hike."

"Did they have camping gear?" Jill asked.

Patton frowned. "I don't recall."

"Most hikers limit their hikes to five hours. If it was six or seven hours down to the lava flow, they would probably have planned to camp and do the return hike the next day."

"Where are you coming up with these numbers?" Patton asked as he sat.

"I was the superintendent of the Wupatki National Monument. We led hiking groups into the park and planned a three-day, two-night backpack trip to hike a fifteen-mile loop." She nodded at me. "Doug and I have made that hike, and we each carried forty pounds of gear, food, and water."

Patton stopped us. "Let me see if Steve Langevin is here. He did the investigation and can better answer your questions." From a radio on his credenza, Patton paged Langevin. A garbled reply followed. "He's just down the road. Would you like a cup of coffee while we wait for him?"

"Sure," I replied.

The coffee pot was in a tiny break room with a refrigerator in the corner. "Help yourself," Patton said as he placed a dollar bill into the slot on top of a can.

"What issues do you have besides dead hikers?" I asked.

"The usual stuff," Patton replied as he poured himself a cup of coffee. "People wander off the trails and kill habitat. Speeders race down the roads and run into the barriers. People take chunks of lava as souvenirs. Things like that."

A slender man with sandy, sun-bleached hair was waiting for us in Patton's office. Accustomed to cops in spit-and-polished uniforms, the weathered shirt and pants worn by this man didn't inspire confidence.

Patton introduced Steve Langevin. "This is Doug Fletcher and his partner, Jill." Patton stopped. "I didn't catch your last name, Jill."

"I'm Jill Fletcher," she said, shaking Langevin's hand.

"How can I help?" Langevin asked, leaning one hip on Patton's desk as the rest of us sat in the remaining chairs.

"We're here to investigate the deaths on the lava flow."

Langevin looked at Patton, then back at us. "It's an open and closed case. The hikers walked past a closed gate, inhaled volcanic laze on the lava flow, then died almost instantly."

"It's a long hike from the gate to the lava flow," I said. "Did it appear they planned to camp there before returning?"

"I think they were planning to walk down and return right away."

Jill stood and pointed to the map. "It's nineteen miles. That's more than a six-hour, one-way walk."

Langevin shrugged. "I guess."

"Did they have camping gear?" I asked.

"Not that I saw."

"How much water were they carrying?" Jill asked.

"I don't recall."

Unable to contain my frustration, I asked. "Where was the hikers' vehicle parked?"

The ranger considered that for a moment. "There wasn't a vehicle parked near the closed gate. Someone must've dropped them off."

"Did the people who dropped them off report them missing?"

"No. They probably heard they were dead and didn't want to be involved."

"Was there anything suspicious about their deaths?" I asked.

"Not really. When people inhale laze, it irritates their lungs. They probably inhaled some concentrated laze and died quickly."

"I didn't see a corrective action plan in your report," Jill said.

Langevin glanced at Patton. "There's a sign on the gate that says, 'road closed.' I suggested a new sign that says, 'If the gate is closed, going past here might kill you.' Mike felt that was over the top."

Jill composed herself before replying. "Perhaps something like, 'Beware of toxic volcanic fumes beyond this point' would be more appropriate."

Langevin shrugged. "That'd work, too."

Patton was shaking his head. "No amount of signage will prevent people from doing stupid things. I thought about installing a six-foot high fence, but we'd need miles of it along the road to block all the possible access points."

I stood. "Can you drive us to the site of the deaths, Steve?"

"There's a Kona wind today, so the Chain of Craters Road is closed. I can drive you to the gate, but that's as close as we can get until the wind changes direction."

"What's the weather forecast for the next few days?" Jill asked.

"They think we'll have trade winds again tomorrow," Langevin replied. "Based on their past accuracy, I'd say there's a fifty-fifty chance we'll open the road tomorrow."

"Did you watch the autopsies, Steve?" I asked.

He shuddered. "Those bodies were so eaten up by the acid, there was no point in watching the pathologist cut them open. Hell, he probably didn't even have to cut. He probably just scooped out the juices."

"What did his report list as the cause of death?" I asked, suspecting that he'd never even read the report.

"I didn't need a doctor to know that those folks died from inhaling the acidic laze."

I couldn't restrain myself any longer. "Ah, it was obvious they hadn't been shot, stabbed, strangled, or beaten to death."

Langevin turned red. "They were found lying on the lava where an acidic cloud had been blowing over their bodies for two days. It didn't take a rocket scientist to figure out what had happened. I believe the pathologist's report agrees with me."

"The pathologist's report wasn't attached to your statement on the Park Service database."

"It didn't arrive until after my report went in."

I glared at Patton. "Your law enforcement ranger didn't attend the post-mortem exam and submitted his report before he had the autopsy results?"

Patton was unruffled. "Accident reports have to be submitted within 48-hours. I asked Steve to submit his report before his days off. Besides, the pathologist concurred with Steve's assessment."

Trying to cool me off, Jill smiled. "Could you make a copy of the coroner's report for us?"

Patton gestured to the ranger. "I don't have a copy." He stood. "Steve can run a copy for you."

Something about Langevin's glance at Patton made my skin prickle. Steve cleared his throat. "It was a verbal report."

"Uh huh," I said. "Not only did you skip the autopsy, you didn't even get a copy of the autopsy report?"

"It might be in my unopened mail."

Jill gestured toward the door. "Let's check." She looked at Patton, who was entering his computer password, content that whatever happened wasn't his problem. "Mike, why don't you join us?"

"I'm sure Steve's got this."

Jill stiffened. "Superintendent Patton, please join us in *your* law enforcement ranger's office."

Patton's eyes narrowed. "I told you, Steve's got what you need."

"You seem to be ignoring the fact that a screw-up by one of your people is *your problem* until it's resolved."

"Listen *Investigator Fletcher,* I'm in charge of this park. You're not my boss. You're not even in my chain of command. If you don't like the way I've dealt with this *accident*, you can tell my boss. My experience is that as long as I'm staying within my budget, I'm meeting my personal metrics."

Jill leaned on the edge of Patton's desk. "Two people died on your watch. That's on you, especially if your law enforcement ranger failed to pursue the investigation with due diligence."

"The hikers disobeyed posted signs and warnings. I am not responsible for peoples' stupidity."

"It will be your problem if we determine that Steve dropped the ball."

"Don't threaten me. I've had an unblemished forty-seven-year US National Park Service career. Close the door when you leave."

Jill was steaming as she followed Steve and me to his tiny office. After unlocking the door and turning on the lights, Steve removed the piles of paper from his two guest chairs. He obviously had few visitors. Based on the dust on top of the piles of paper, I also assumed he wasn't into housekeeping.

"The report should be in this pile," he said, lifting a one-inch-thick pile of unopened envelopes from the corner of his desk. After flipping through them and not finding what he wanted, he pushed around the papers spread across the desktop. "Maybe I opened it and got distracted."

"Maybe Doug and I should walk around the caldera overlook while you dig through the piles," Jill said.

Steve tossed papers from the chairs onto the desktop, adding to the disarray. "I probably threw the report away when I saw that it confirmed my suspicion."

"I'll call the coroner and get a copy," Jill said.

Langevin shrugged. "Do whatever you need to do." He checked his watch. "I need to drive down to the Chain of Craters Road to make sure no one has broken the lock and opened the gate."

"We'll ride with you," Jill offered.

"Nah, I'm driving home from there. I'll have one of the interpretive rangers take you down to the lava flow when the wind changes."

I followed Jill from the visitor center to the parking lot. She was uncharacteristically quiet when we got into the rental pickup. "That was useless," I said, starting the engine.

"They don't care."

I backed out of the parking spot and turned toward the caldera loop road. "They have an answer that fits their preconceived ideas."

"Do you think Jack knows how poorly Langevin investigated?"

"He might not know, but he suspects that their investigation was less than rigorous."

I parked at the Kilauea Crater overlook. We leaned on the railing overlooking the steaming caldera. Jill blew out a breath. "I wonder how many times I've accepted a ranger's incomplete analysis of an accident?"

"You're perceptive enough to know when someone's blowing smoke up your butt."

Jill turned slightly toward me, and a smile curled her lips. "I am now. I'm not so sure I would've picked up on that when I was a superintendent."

"That's true. I blew smoke up your butt every time we spoke about the Walnut Canyon investigation."

"YOU DID NOT!"

I pulled her into a hug. "You're right. I respected you too much to lie to you, even when Jamie and I thought we'd hit a dead end."

"What did you once tell me about integrity?"

"That's a C.S. Lewis quote. 'Integrity is doing the right thing, even when no one is watching.'"

"You have integrity, Fletcher."

"How do you know what I do when no one is watching?"

"You may be cynical, but you have integrity. You've never lied to me."

"That's pushing it. I may have told a white lie once in a while to protect you from the truth."

Jill pushed me away to arms length. "What? When have you told me a white lie?"

"I might've overstated the extent of my knee injury when you wanted me to investigate the

Walnut Canyon murder. I hoped you'd find someone else to take over the investigation."

"Your knee *is* gimpy."

"Maybe not as gimpy as I told you."

"I may have lied about my horsemanship."

"What?"

"I told you I was riding as soon as I could reach the stirrups."

"That wasn't true?"

"I was riding before I could reach the stirrups."

"I think we should visit the pathologist before we get into another discussion about moving to South Dakota."

"We *are* moving to the Black Hills…someday," Jill whispered as a young couple walked past.

I released my hug and stepped toward the pickup. "We need to talk to the pathologist."

Chapter 6

The smiling volunteer at the hospital reception desk called the pathologist who'd performed the autopsies, then directed us to Dr. Nakamura's office, deep in the bowels of the building. My knock on the pathologist's door interrupted whatever he was doing on the computer. Smiling, he stood and extended his hand. "The Fletchers, I presume."

"Jill and Doug," I said.

Gesturing for us to take seats at a small conference table, Nakamura sat across from us. "What can I do for the National Park Service?"

"We understand you did the post-mortem exam on the bodies found on the lava flow."

Nakamura turned and lifted a folder from his desk, he then handed it to Jill. "Here's a copy for you. Is there something more you'd like to know?"

As Jill opened the folder and started re-reading the first page I replied, "Ranger Langevin seems to have misplaced his copy of your report."

"I filed a copy with the South Hawaii County police. One of their people probably gave a copy to the Park Service."

I leaned forward. "Being a cop who's seen a fair number of autopsies, I know that pathologists and medical examiners make observations that aren't included in the report. What can you tell us besides what we've read?"

The doctor smiled. "My unrecorded observations and opinions are usually left out because they're not substantiated by fact and chemistry."

Jill looked up from the report. "They're the things you wouldn't like to defend on the witness stand."

"Correct."

"I understand," I said, leaning on my elbows, "but we'd like to have some additional threads that might lead us to other evidence."

Steepling his fingers, Nakamura leaned back. "I don't want to be quoted."

"Agreed. We're off the record."

"I've only seen body trauma like those people experienced one other time. A stupid kid tried a Jackie Chan trick. He jumped off a hotel balcony, planning to bounce off the canopy over a sidewalk café, then land on his feet in the street."

Nodding, I said, "And there was no bounce in the canopy."

"None at all. He went straight through the canvas and hit the concrete sidewalk between two tables. Scared the hell out of the diners and ruined their meals."

Jill shook her head. "Let me guess; alcohol was involved."

"Yeah, I heard someone submitted his stunt for a Darwin Award. You know, the internet award for the stupidest tricks that remove a victim from the gene pool, so his stupidity isn't passed on to another generation."

"How were his injuries similar to those of the bodies recovered from the lava?" I asked.

"The couple found on the lava had fallen from a height that splintered their femurs and compressed their spines. Their hearts continued to beat long enough for them to inhale volcanic laze. The acid and glass particles in the laze caused their lungs to fill with fluid."

Jill flipped open the autopsy report. "You said they died of pneumonia asphyxiation."

"They would've died from their traumatic injuries if the pneumonia hadn't killed them first."

"You didn't include any observations about the death scene," I said.

"I never saw the bodies in situ. They were delivered to me in an ambulance."

"Who declared them dead?"

The doctor chuckled. "Considering their state of decomposition, there was little question that they were deceased when discovered. I signed the death certificate, but your people and the ambulance crew were correct in assuming that life saving measures weren't required."

"How long had the bodies been on the lava before they were found?" Jill asked.

"My initial external exam made me think they'd been dead for more than a week. Their skin was black and puckered."

"But that's not your final determination?"

"Having done autopsies for decades, I know there's a distinctive odor to a rotting corpse. Those two bodies were being dissolved by the acid in the volcanic steam and fog. Based on the limited decomposition of their internal organs, I estimated that they'd been dead less than twenty-four hours."

Jill opened the file and quickly flipped through the pages. "You didn't include death scene photos."

"None were supplied to me."

"Is that common?" I asked.

Shifting uncomfortably, the doctor paused. "The county police usually supply me with photos of the death scene before I write the autopsy report."

"But none were supplied with these bodies," I said.

"No."

"Would you like to speculate on the reason you weren't given photos?"

"Not really. I mean, pictures may have been taken that weren't provided to me. I can't say why."

"Do you know the proximity of the bodies to a cliff or some tall structure?" Jill asked.

"Having not been at the death scene, and not having photos, I have no way of knowing."

"For all you know, they could've been dropped from a plane," I said.

"That's certainly within the realm of possibility. Lacking any facts beyond my examination of the corpses, I'm unable to do anything but hypothesize."

Staring at the diplomas on the office wall, I asked, "Can you speculate on the deaths at all?"

Nakamura snorted. "I could speculate all day, but anything I said would be exactly that; pure speculation."

"Where would you suggest we start our investigation?" Jill asked.

"I don't think anyone in law enforcement ever found the decedents' lodgings. It would be interesting to know if their hotel room was on the sixth floor of a hotel."

Jill cocked her head. "The sixth floor? Not higher?"

"I think the tallest hotel on the Big Island is six stories high."

"Do you think their injuries could've been caused by a six-story fall?"

"I'd say six stories would be about right."

"Maybe they fell off a cliff near a waterfall," Jill suggested.

"We can sit here and speculate all day," Nakamura said. "The reality is, we'll likely never know with a high degree of certainty what happened unless you find a witness to their fall. Offhand, I'd say it's likely that their injuries would've killed them long before anyone could've transported them from a Kona hotel or a waterfall to the lava field where they died."

"Could they have been assaulted where they were found?" Jill asked.

"That's certainly a possibility," Nakamura said. "In my professional opinion, their fractures were caused by a fall, not a beating. The type of bone fractures they suffered aren't associated with blunt force trauma."

"What else might've caused them besides a fall?" Jill asked.

Nakamura considered his comments before replying, "A massive car accident, a plane crash…" He paused, then added, "but neither of those would cause these types of femoral fractures."

"Was there anything else odd about the bodies?" I asked. "Maybe some unusual fibers or material?"

"They died where they fell. The clothing on the underside of the bodies wasn't attacked by the acidic fog, and the livor mortis was present on the side away from the acid attack. I didn't pick up any trace evidence from the clothes, well, aside from lava grit."

"No defensive injuries?" I asked.

"None that I saw."

"Did you find any skin or fibers in the fingernail scrapings?" I asked.

Nakamura's expression changed. "The woman's fingernails were torn, like she grabbed onto something before her fall. There wasn't any skin under her nails, which leads me to believe they weren't broken while fending off an attacker."

"And her male companion?"

"That was odd. His fingernails were intact."

"So, the woman tried to grab something before she fell, but the man didn't. Do you think he was drugged or unconscious?"

"I don't have the toxicology results back, so I can't comment on drug or alcohol impairment. As for consciousness, the severe trauma he suffered made it hard to determine if he'd been struck on his head before his skull hit the lava."

"If you had to guess…"

Nakamura frowned at me. "I don't guess. The science and evidence are either there, or they aren't."

Jill redirected the questions before I offended the doctor. "You identified the man based on the ID in his wallet, correct?"

"His drivers license, and credit cards gave me a preliminary identification. I confirmed his identity with dental records."

"How did you ID the woman?"

"I couldn't make a preliminary ID because all she was carrying was a smashed cell phone. I called the man's employer. They advised me that the victims had been out of contact with the office while on a remote assignment. They supplied her name and address, which allowed me to acquire her dental records."

"The news that the two victims were co-workers wasn't supplied to us by the investigating ranger. Who was their employer and what were their jobs?"

"They were photojournalists from a Honolulu public relations firm. He took photos. She documented the shots and got releases from people in the photos."

Jill paused. "If she was documenting the photos and getting releases for use of images, I'd expect her to have a computer, an iPad, or a backpack with paperwork. None of those things were delivered to you with the bodies?"

"Like I said, all that arrived here were her body, phone, and clothing."

"What were they working on at the time of their deaths?"

"The company didn't have details of their activities. They had an assignment to take Big Island photos to be used in promotional literature. They had free rein to find any scenes or landscapes that would attract tourists."

I took out a notebook. "Where were they staying?"

"The company doesn't book rooms for them. The manager I spoke with said he rarely knew about their accommodations until their travel vouchers were submitted."

Looking at Jill I asked, "Their employer said the man was a photographer. I don't remember Steve mentioning a camera found with the bodies."

"He didn't. Maybe they weren't working."

The doctor frowned. "I've never met a professional photographer who didn't have at least one camera with him all the time. They often carry two."

Jill opened the file with the autopsy results. "How long did they live after the fall?"

Nakamura frowned. "That would require speculation."

"Did they suffer?"

Having heard that question a hundred or more times from the families of car crash victims, I knew that the politically correct answer was, "they died immediately." I expected the doctor to respond with that reassuring lie.

I was surprised when Nakamura said, "They were probably unconscious from the impact, but they lived long enough to inhale the acidic fog. Their lungs immediately responded to the acid and glass particles by filling with fluid that drowned them. They lived no more than five minutes before their hearts stopped beating."

"But they were unconscious. Right?"

"Probably."

Jill surprised me when she stood. "I'd like to see the woman's body."

Nakamura remained seated. "I don't think that would be a good idea. Between the impact and the acid attack on their tissues, the bodies aren't…"

I stood. "Is there a medical reason we can't see the bodies?"

"No," the doctor said as he rose. "They're…unpleasant."

"We're law enforcement officers, Doctor. Not family members."

"I've completed my examinations. There's nothing to see."

"Are the bodies still here?" I asked.

"I won't release them until the toxicology results are back. So, yes, they're here."

"Let's walk to the morgue."

After gesturing toward his door, the doctor led us down a hallway to a locked door he opened by holding his ID card to a reader. The morgue looked like any other autopsy suite, with a stainless-steel table in the center of the room and a row of metal cabinets securing the refrigerated remains. Taking gloves and masks from containers mounted inside the door, the doctor led us to a cabinet door with a small card that simply read, *Jane Doe*.

"I haven't added their names to the cards," he said as he pulled on the latch causing a rack to slide out, exposing a body covered by a light green sheet. "This isn't going to be pretty. No mortician has prepared the bodies."

Stepping past the doctor, Jill pulled back the sheet with her gloved hand. As we'd been warned, the woman's head was misshapen due to the impact, and her skin darkened by the acid. Her hair and exposed teeth were the only features making the woman's head recognizable as a human being. Pulling the sheet back farther, Jill exposed the woman's torso, showing the crude stitches used to close her chest after the pathologist made the Y incision to access her internal organs.

"Her chest isn't black," Jill said, staring at the purple mottled skin of the woman's exposed torso.

"Her torso was protected from the acid by the canvas vest she wore."

Jill's eyes drifted to the woman's decomposed left hand. "Was she wearing a wedding ring?"

"She was wearing a watch, but no other jewelry except for gold stud earrings. The gold earrings were the only items not attacked by the acidic laze."

Jill lifted the corpse's left hand and examined the blackened fingers. "The victim was into function not beauty. Her fingernails were polished, but she didn't have a professional manicure. And you're right, I can see that she was apparently clawing for a grip on something. Her nails are chipped and broken off halfway to the cuticle." Pulling the sheet over the body, Jill asked, "Was there anything else unusual about your external examination?"

"Not really. The male victim wore jeans and a t-shirt. The woman was wearing shorts, a t-shirt, and a canvas vest. Any organic evidence, like fibers, was degraded by the acid laze." The doctor paused as something occurred to him. "There was one thing; the woman had coarse black sand particles in the heels of her hands and ground into her knees. It was almost as if she'd been crawling on the black sand beach."

"Is there a specific black sand beach you had in mind?" I asked.

"There's a famous black sand beach at the southern tip of this island. The granules are large, making it uncomfortable for walking in bare feet, so it's not a swimming destination."

"How far is that beach from the lava flow where the bodies were found?" I asked.

"It's miles away — maybe a forty-five-minute drive."

"Were there sand particles on the man's knees, too?" Jill asked.

The doctor sighed. "No. There were particles embedded in the soles of both pairs of shoes, but the man's hands and knees were devoid of sand particles."

The doctor slid the body back into the cooler. "There was a cell phone, a digital recorder, and a few dollars in the woman's pockets."

"Did you recover any calls or data from the recorder or cell phone?" I asked.

"They're still with her clothing. I don't have the capability to do that analysis."

Jill frowned. "The police didn't take them?"

"The bodies were delivered by two EMTs in an ambulance. I haven't seen either the police or the investigating ranger. Neither agency requested anything but the autopsy report."

I looked at the doctor in disbelief. "Neither the Park Service nor the local police took their phones for analysis?"

"No. Both the man and the woman's phones are with the remnants of their clothing. Both phones are in tough shape from the impact, but no one has asked about them."

"We'd like to take them with us," I said. "Where are you storing them?"

"They're in boxes on the shelf, over here."

I followed the doctor across the room. "Is this room secure? Who else has access to it?"

"You saw that I had to use my chip card to get in. So, it's not accessible to the public."

"Who else's chip will open the autopsy room door?"

Nakamura turned. "You're concerned that someone may have tampered with the phones?"

"At this point, I hope that the phones are still here. My secondary concern is that you're storing evidence in an unsecured space. Who else can access this room?"

The doctor pulled two covered banker's boxes down from a shelf and set them on a counter. "I suppose all the professional staff have chip cards that would open the door to this room. It's not like we're concerned about someone stealing bodies."

I opened the closest box and looked at a handwritten list of the contents. Shoes, shirt, jeans, phone, wallet, watch, and SDXC memory card. I removed a zippered plastic bag and held it out to the doctor. "Did you seal this when you put it in the box?"

"I…assume I did."

Pulling out the wallet, I unfolded it, exposing empty credit card slots and an empty cash flap. "Were there cash and credit cards in the wallet when you placed it in storage?"

The doctor's face reddened. "There were credit cards. I didn't look for cash."

I glanced around the room. "There aren't any security cameras in this area?"

"Umm…no."

Setting the wallet into the box, I lifted out another bag. The cell phone was misshapen, and the screen was spider-webbed with cracks. I pushed aside the degraded clothing and shoes. "There isn't a watch or memory card in the box." Putting the cell phone back into the bag I asked again. "Who else can get in here? Is there a janitor?"

"Of course, there's a janitor. I don't clean…" Nakamura froze, his mind considering a list of the people who may have accessed the room. "Aw shit. I think there's a security camera at each end of the hallway."

"Who monitors them?" I asked.

"I assume the security officers do."

"Take me to the security director's office."

* * *

Finding the security director's office unoccupied, Nakamura unlocked the room where security cameras displayed views of the hallways, entrances, and exits. The room had two unoccupied chairs.

"They don't monitor the security cameras?" Jill asked.

Nakamura shrugged. "I'm not sure."

"Who is the boss?" I asked.

"The hospital administrator has overall responsibility for the hospital's operation. He reports to a hospital board of local officials."

Nakamura led us to the administrator's office. I opened the door without knocking. The six people sitting around the conference table looked up when I entered the room with Jill and Dr. Nakamura on my heels.

A chunky middle-aged man with his tie loose and the top button of his shirt undone stood, "We're in the middle of a meeting. Please speak with my administrative assistant if you'd like to schedule a meeting with me."

Sliding my badge forward on my belt so everyone could see it, I said, "There's been a security breach in the autopsy suite and evidence has been removed."

The man stared at me for a second, then looked past me at the pathologist. "I'm sure our security director would be happy to meet with you and Dr. Nakamura to discuss this *alleged* breach at a later time."

I unclipped and held up my badge as I approached the table. "I'm a federal law enforcement officer investigating two suspicious deaths. Evidence has been removed from what should be a secure room inside this hospital."

A man who looked like he might've once been a college basketball player stood and gestured toward the door. "Let's take this to my office."

"Are you the CEO?" I asked. "Because this hospital seems to have systemic security issues that should probably lead to the firing of whomever is in charge."

The tall man's face turned red, and he balled his fists. "I'm the security director. As I said, let's take this to my office."

I looked at the man with the dangling tie, the only person in the room not in casual attire. "Are you the CEO of this circus?"

The man in the tie sat down and grabbed a box of tissues. "I'm Craig Halvor, the hospital president. You're interrupting a meeting."

"I'm reporting a crime that took place in your hospital, and I don't really care if I'm intruding on your meeting. This hospital is a security nightmare, and it's *your* problem."

Halvor picked up the tissue box and squeezed it as if trying to strangle it. "Your comments are out of line. I suggest you leave with Ted." Relaxing his grip on the tissues he said, "I'm sure Ted can deal with whatever perceived security problems you have."

I walked past the security director and got into the CEO's face. "The lack of security cameras in secure areas, the excessive number of people with access to secured areas, and the absence of anyone monitoring what few security cameras you have is hardly a 'perceived' problem.' I assume this is your operating committee. Let's get them all involved because this isn't the security director's problem. Who was the janitor last night? We need to compare his or her fingerprints to the fingerprints on an evidence box and the plastic bag that contained the victim's wallet and watch…before his cash, watch, and credit cards were stolen from the morgue."

The CEO crushed the tissue box in his hands. "Ted, remove this man from the room and hold him until the Hawaii County police get here."

I stared at Ted as he took a step toward me. "If you touch me, I'll arrest you for assaulting a federal officer in the line of duty and interfering with a felony investigation. I believe that is a level C felony which means you'll spend at least three years in prison, and you'll never have a security job again."

The security man stopped and stared at my sidearm. "Craig, I think we need to listen to this man's complaint."

The man in the tie started to speak, "I asked you to…"

"This isn't a local cop you can brush aside, Craig. This guy is a federal agent. If his allegations of theft from the morgue are true, we have a problem."

The CEO looked at me. "I'll speak with you after this meeting."

I pulled out an empty chair and sat. "You'll deal with us now. Or, I can take you into custody, have you transported to the federal holding facility in

Honolulu where you can call your lawyer, and we'll talk there. It's up to you."

He looked toward a woman wearing a visitor badge and typing into a laptop. "Can he do that, Candace?"

The woman stopped typing and cleared her throat. "As the hospital general consul, I believe that's within his power if he perceives that you're interfering with or delaying a federal investigation."

"Are we talking here and now, or later in Honolulu, Craig?"

The CEO gestured to the other meeting participants. "Let's reconvene in fifteen minutes."

"Actually, I think you want these people to be part of this discussion. Some of them may be complicit in the theft of federal evidence if they're aware of insufficient security protocols and failed to act."

A woman who looked like a person accustomed to heavy labor, probably the head of housekeeping, stood and asked, "What?"

"Anyone who knew that the security measures were inadequate, that you failed to screen your employees, or insufficiently secured the contents of the morgue but failed to address it, is complicit in this theft."

Candace, the lawyer nodded. "I suggest that we table the security discussion while Ted assists the federal officer. What is your name and title, sir?"

"I'm Investigator Douglas Fletcher from the National Park Service Investigative Services Branch. My partner and I have been assigned to investigate the death of the two people in Dr.

Nakamura's morgue. While checking the victim's belongings, we discovered that several items were logged and placed into storage boxes but are now missing."

The lawyer looked to the security director. "I suggest you assist Investigator Fletcher as best you can without interjecting any subjective comments about the hospital's security."

I looked around the room. "My concerns about stolen evidence should be addressed, but aren't all of you concerned about the safety of your staff and patients?"

A woman wearing an ID tag with RN printed after her name put her hands flat on the table. "Dammit, Craig, you've cut our budgets to the bone, and now look at what's happened." She glared at the security director. "Ted, tell the investigator why there isn't anyone watching the security monitors."

The lawyer cleared her throat. "Now is neither the time nor place to be airing our laundry."

Ted, the security director, sat and drew a breath. "Candace, the security situation is hardly dirty laundry. My budget only provides for coverage of the cameras during the night shift."

The lawyer ended the discussion. "Let's comply with the officer's request without airing opinions and petty grievances."

"Can we see the security video from the last three days?" I asked.

"I'm not sure the video quality will be sufficient to identify anyone. The cameras record analog photos that we convert to digital data for storage.

There is no video, per se, just a series of grainy photos that are taken every five seconds."

Nakamura snorted. "Do you mean the gas station has better security cameras than the Hilo hospital?"

The security director looked toward the lawyer to see if she was going to block his reply. She nodded her approval to respond but he carefully weighed his response. "We have security people on site 24/7 and we have images from the security cameras. We don't have digital video cameras. Video equipment upgrades are included in my current budget request."

"This is neither the time, nor the place to be airing our budgetary issues," the CEO said. He turned to me. "What would you like to ask me…us?"

"To start with, who had access to the morgue besides Dr. Nakamura?"

Clearing his throat, the security director stared at the CEO. "We have general access control that requires our employees to use their ID badges to open secure doors. Anyone with a chip in their ID cards can access virtually any interior or exterior door, day or night."

"Does that include former employees?" I asked.

The CEO leaned forward. "We take the badges of all employees who quit."

"How about the employees who just stop showing up for work; do you go to their houses to take their badges, or do you reprogram the system, so they no longer have access?"

The lawyer looked at Ted in a way that indicated he shouldn't answer. Then she smiled at me. "That functionality will be part of our next round of security upgrades."

The nurse pointed her finger at the CEO. "Ted's proposed security upgrades were removed from the last budget and they're red-lined in the current proposed budget." She looked at me. "Pull the minutes from our last budget meeting before Craig erases them."

Candace closed her laptop. "Our budget plans are not part of this discussion. We won't provide those meeting minutes without a search warrant. That said, I can personally assure the officers that no records will be erased or modified." She looked around the room. "This is now a police matter. Our records are frozen. Do not delete or shred anything."

I looked at a man in a Hawaiian shirt who'd suddenly become interested in a hangnail. "What's your position?"

"Me?" he asked, looking surprised. "I'm the chief medical officer."

"Ah, so you're the one who's responsible for securing the medications and the surgical suites. Are they protected so no one can walk off with a bottle of oxycontin or enter a surgical suite during an operation?"

The security director interrupted by saying, "All the scheduled narcotics, nuclear medicines, and chemo drugs are kept under lock and key. The surgical suites are a separate security zone accessible only by the surgical staff, pharmacists, and a limited number of housekeeping people."

"Are those areas under 24/7 video surveillance?" Jill asked.

"There's video surveillance, but no one monitors the displays except on night shift when there aren't hospital staff members around."

Holding up her hand to end the conversation, the lawyer looked at me. "Specifically, what do you need for your investigation of the missing items?"

"I need to know who accessed the morgue and removed the victim's belongings."

The CEO struggled to contain his anger, ripping the tissue box nearly in half, the tissues spilling onto the conference table. He was about to speak when the lawyer cut off his reply. "Ted, can you pull up the video of the hallways and the electronic record of whose IDs have opened the morgue in the past three days for the officers?"

Nodding, the security director said, "The hospital security system is split into zones, by floor. I can get records of anyone who entered any secure room in the zone that includes the morgue."

"Is that sufficient?" the lawyer asked.

"It's a start. I'll also need the background checks you ran on those employees, along with copies of their fingerprints."

"We only do background checks on the doctors, nurses, and pharmacists," Ted replied as he stood. He looked at the CEO. "It costs too much to check all the housekeeping applicants, lab techs, nurses' aides, cooks…or the security officers."

The lawyer interrupted the reply and walked to the door while the CEO seethed. "Let's excuse the security director from our meeting so he can comply with the specific requests of our guests."

She pulled the director aside and whispered something to him as Nakamura, Jill, and I passed.

We followed Ted out of the meeting room. An argument broke out behind us as the door closed. "Thank you," the security director said as he gestured for us to walk toward his office. "I've been suggesting security upgrades since I arrived four years ago. There's always something more pressing than security cameras or upgrades to the card control system. I think you were able to get Craig's attention better than I've been able to."

"What's with the CEO and the tissue box?" Jill asked.

The pathologist chuckled. "Craig is undergoing anger management counselling. The tissue box helps him sublimate his anger in a less harmful manner."

"Less harmful?" Jill asked.

The security director nodded. "Craig doesn't throw pens, staplers, waste baskets, or chairs anymore."

"That's terrible," Jill replied. "Why is he still in charge?"

"Craig won't be the CEO if the hospital board has to replace another window because he threw a chair through it," Nakamura said as he bid us goodbye.

Jill fell into step alongside me. "You came on a little strong in there, Doug."

"I'm irritated, sleep deprived, my blood sugar is crashing, and I'm sick of bureaucrats playing budgetary games."

"You could try to play nice once in a while."

"Not this time. If I hadn't made a scene, we'd be waiting outside the CEO's office until he felt like talking to us. He needed to be taken down a notch, and hearing the input from the other directors and the lawyer was…enlightening. We may have to find out who certifies hospitals and determine the security requirements for certification."

Jill smirked. "I think the tissue box the CEO ripped apart was a sublimation that kept him from wringing your neck."

Chapter 7

Ted took a keychain from his pocket and unlocked his office. Intrigued by his choice to use a keyed lock rather than the electronic security system, I asked, "Do you need to lock your office? You don't rely on the card control system?"

He gestured for us to sit in the two guest chairs. "I know how messed up some of the security is. All the directors rely on mechanical door locks so no one can walk in by scanning their ID badge. We all have confidential information like personnel files, that we need to be kept secure from general access."

Jill pressed her fingertips against her forehead as if she had a sudden headache. "I wonder if the Rapid City hospital has better security than Hilo…"

Ted chuckled as he logged onto his computer. "Ma'am, I can assure you that almost any major hospital has better security systems than we have."

Jill leaned forward in her chair. "If we're cooperating in the investigation, please call me Jill. My jetlagged, tired, hot-headed partner goes by Doug."

Without turning away from his computer task, the security director said, "Are you doing a good cop/bad cop thing, or are we really working together on this?"

After giving me a warning look, Jill replied, "We're Park Service investigators, not cops. We don't do the good cop/bad cop thing. I'm always pleasant and my partner is a cynical ex-detective who's often grumpy."

I mouthed *grumpy?* Jill smiled and nodded.

Ted turned his chair. "You two work for the Park Service? In the conference room you said you were federal law enforcement officers. I thought you were probably US Marshals."

"We're Park Service investigators out of Padre Island, Texas. Like the FBI or marshals service, we're federal law enforcement officers. When required, we wear bullet-proof vests with a 'Federal Police' logo."

"The Park Service has its own investigators?"

Jill held out her credentials and said, "We are part of the National Park Service Investigative Services Bureau. We investigate suspicious deaths and disappearances in National Park properties."

"Your headquarters are in Texas, not Washington D.C.?"

"We reside in Texas and are dispatched wherever we're required. There aren't that many of us, and our counterparts are spread across the country."

"Whew! You're a long way from Texas."

I cut Jill off. "We're currently assigned to investigate the deaths of the two hikers who died in Volcanoes National Park."

"The news said they died from inhaling the volcanic laze."

"Technically, pneumonia was their cause of death. Inhaled hydrochloric acid and glass particles from laze were contributing factors. The Park Service would like to understand the events leading to the discovery of their bodies on the lava flow."

"I get it. I have to investigate and develop a corrective action plan after every employee or patient accident."

"Exactly," Jill replied. "We need to know the events leading to their deaths so future deaths can be prevented."

Ted turned to his computer. "Okay, I'll print a list of the people who accessed doors in the basement security zone during the past seventy-two hours." After a series of keystrokes his printer came to life and a spreadsheet fed out of a slot.

Jill scanned the list as Ted turned back to the computer and pulled up a grainy black and white image. "Dr. Nakamura's name shows up on half the lines."

"That's not surprising," Ted replied, turning his computer monitor so it was visible to Jill and me. "Other than the morgue, the security zone I'm showing you is just building facilities."

"Facilities?" I asked.

"Yeah, like the air conditioning, plumbing, electrical panels, and the piping for the oxygen and nitrogen gasses that are stored in bulk tanks outside. I expect that the other half of the people making door entries are the janitors, electricians, and plumbers."

"Let's look at the security camera images to see who, besides the pathologist, accessed the morgue."

"This could take a while. We're going to spend a lot of time staring at an empty hallway."

Jill pushed the printout showing the access points back to the security director. "Can you fast forward to 8:13 two nights ago?"

"Sure." After a few keystrokes, the video displayed the time and date as it flipped through grainy images. At precisely 8:12 PM a male figure appeared in the hallway, and a minute later he disappeared into a door on the right side of the screen. "That's the night-shift electrician walking into the room with the hospital's electrical panels and HVAC controls."

With her finger following the corresponding line on the printout, Jill said, "He exits seven minutes later. The next entry is 10:23."

Ted sped through grainy images of the empty hallway until a man pushing a janitorial cart appeared. The janitor scanned his card and entered to clean the morgue.

"How long was he inside?" I asked.

"He exited at 10:44," Jill replied. "It seems reasonable that it took him twenty minutes to clean and mop the morgue."

"The cynical cop in me says that's also plenty of time to open boxes and remove credit cards and cash from the victim's wallet."

The security director sighed. "If the janitor is the only person other than the pathologist who goes in and out of the morgue, we'll have to question him."

An HVAC man entered the facility room at 2:07 AM and left four minutes later. "The next entry is 8:17 AM." Again, the grainy pictures sped by.

"Back up!"

Ted stopped when the counter said 6:43. "The log said no one used an access card until 8:17."

"Back up," I said. "There was a flash of someone in the hallway."

We watched grainy images of the hallway, with the counter rolling backwards until 5:02. "There! Someone's walking away from the camera. Keep going back."

Ted stopped the display at 5:01. "Damn, he's coming out of the morgue."

"Jill, who opened the morgue door at 5:01?" I asked.

"No one. There's no record of anyone opening a door in this security zone at that time."

Ted continued backing up until we saw the person halfway into the morgue door at 4:53. Jill looked at the printout. "There's no record of any door in the basement zone being opened by a card at that time?"

Ted froze the images, one at a time, freezing the person coming down the hallway. Pictures of the hallway jerked ahead every five seconds. "That person isn't in uniform. It must be someone who's changed into civvies or someone from outside the hospital."

"How did he open the morgue door without a digital record?" I asked.

Ted leaned back and wiped the perspiration from his forehead with his hand. "I don't know. I suppose someone could slip a metal strip into the lock and open the door."

Jill looked at me. "Didn't I once hear you say the term *ghetto key*, Doug?"

"That's throwing a brick through a window to get into a car," I said. "I think this guy used a credit card like a *slim jim* to push the latch aside."

"I didn't see him holding anything," the security director said. "On the other hand, a lot could've happened in the five seconds between frames."

As Ted scrolled the frames back and forth, I looked at the person in the hallway. His or her upper face was hidden by a hoodie sweatshirt with an indecipherable logo on the right chest. The person's pants were dark jeans, and shoes without any visible logo.

"Do you recognize that person, Ted?" I asked.

"Between the poor picture quality and the hoodie, that could be my mother for all I know."

"Where was your mother the night of this video?"

Ted's head snapped around to look at me. Seeing my smile, he relaxed. "I don't think that's one of our employees. Most of them wear ID cards on a lanyard that hangs from their neck."

"Can you pull up video of the exterior doors for the time immediately before and after this person went into the morgue?"

"Sure," Ted replied. The image on the screen shifted to the front entryway. "We lock up at ten, so there's no one at the front desk."

The unchanging image of the lobby ran by in five second intervals without ever showing a person in the frame. Ted switched the hallways leading from external exits, and again we saw no one enter or leave.

"Where else could someone get into the hospital?" I asked.

"The ER is open 24 hours, but I have a security guard at the desk overnight."

"Pull up that video, please," Jill said.

The video of the ER waiting area showed a security guard sitting at a desk. His motions appeared jerky because of the five second interval between frames. The entry door opened, and five seconds later there was a uniformed cop crossing the lobby, escorting a man to the security officer. The person with the cop appeared to be wearing the same hoodie and jeans as the person who entered the morgue. "What time is this?" I asked.

"This scene is twelve minutes before the morgue entry."

The cop talked to the security guard. "The hoodie man is walking out of the screen," I said. "He doesn't appear to be escorted."

"He's probably going to use the toilet." Ted replied.

Jill leaned close. "Or he slipped down to the morgue while the cop distracted your security guard. Is there a log of who was in the ER that night?"

"Every admission is logged in," Ted replied as he moved to a different computer. After a few keystrokes, he was in a database with lines of dates, times, names, diagnoses, and treating physicians. "There's no record of any admissions that night aside from a guy who sliced his hand open on a broken bar glass just before midnight."

"Who was your security guard?"

"That's Ed Ohana. He likes working the midnight shift, so he's at the ER desk ten nights every two weeks."

"Do you recognize the cop?" Jill asked.

"It looks like Steve Langevin, although I wouldn't bet my pension on that ID."

Jill straightened and played dumb. "Isn't he a ranger, too?"

"Yeah, he's a part-time cop and part-time park ranger. I think he only works at the park during the tourist season."

"Can you contact Ed Ohana to verify that it was Langevin?" Jill asked.

"He might be asleep. But, yeah, I'll give him a call."

Ohana answered the phone immediately, sounding wide awake. Ted put him on speakerphone and explained that Jill and I were listening on the speaker.

"Ed, we're looking at security footage from two nights ago. A cop came into the ER with someone. Do you remember them?"

"Sure. There's so little happening most nights that anyone coming into the ER is memorable. The cop was Steve Langevin. He came in with a guy he introduced as one of his confidential informants. The informant needed to use the restroom, so Steve and I bullshitted to kill time while the guy used the toilet."

I leaned toward the phone. "Did Langevin mention the informant's name?"

"Steve made it seem like it was a confidential thing, so I didn't ask."

"Did you recognize the informant?"

Ohana chuckled. "Hilo is a small town. You run into most everyone at one time or another. I don't know his name, but I've seen him working at the car wash."

Ted looked between Jill and me. "Any other questions?"

"Was the informant carrying anything when he returned to the waiting room?" I asked.

Ohana paused. "I didn't notice anything in his hands, but he was wearing that bulky hoodie. He could've had a Christmas ham in his pocket, and I wouldn't have seen it. He was acting strange, though. He nodded to Langevin when he got back to the desk, as if saying he was done. I thought he was thanking Steve for getting him to the bathroom, but now that I think about it, that was an odd gesture."

"Thanks, Ed. I'm sorry to interrupt your time off."

"No problem." Ted was reaching for the button to end the call when Ed added, "There was something odd about the informant, Ted. It was like seventy-five degrees outside, and that guy was wearing a heavy hoodie as if he was on top of Mauna Loa in a snowstorm. At first, I thought maybe it was his *look*. You know how teens are with their drooping pants and backwards baseball caps. That guy was sweating like a glass of iced tea. There was something more going on."

"Thanks for that additional information, Ed."

"What's up, Ted? Is that kid in some kind of trouble?"

Ted looked toward me, waiting to see if I was willing to share more information. "Ed, this is Doug Fletcher. Some evidence was stolen from the morgue the night the informant and Officer Langevin visited the ER. The security cameras captured the image of someone in a hoodie accessing the morgue door without using an access card."

"Aw shit," Ohana said. "I thought that guy looked suspicious. I should've kept a better eye on him."

"I appreciate your concern, Mr. Ohana. The blame is on Officer Langevin for escorting the guy into the ER and distracting you."

After disconnecting the call, Ted looked at us. "Now what?"

I stood and put out my hand. "I think our pickup needs a car wash."

"Would you guys send my boss an email highlighting the key security upgrades we should install to maintain patient safety and facility security?"

"Won't that put your job in jeopardy?" Jill asked.

"It might in the short term, but I've documented the need for all the corrections you spoke about. If I get fired because of this, I'll find a good employment lawyer…and a reporter."

After shaking hands with Ted, Jill and I walked out of the hospital. "Do you think Ted will get fired for what he showed us?"

"If you write a succinct summary of our observations and include comments about the reaction of the other department heads and the CEO, I think the hot potato will land in the right place."

Jill stopped. "Me?"

"You're the one who writes the concise recaps of our investigations. I just cut and paste what you write into my reports and hit send."

Jill rushed to keep up with me. "I could teach you how to make your reports less wordy…and violent."

"It'd be a waste of time, like when you tried to teach me how to paint the house trim. It's easier for you to do it than to teach me."

"You were being an obstinate ass."

"We each have our talents. Why try to teach me how to write a sentence without dangling the participle when you do it so well."

"You are infuriating," Jill said as she stepped into the pickup.

"I'm just a realist. I have no interest in learning how to write a brief report when I'm married to the master."

"Don't try to butter me up…"

"Do you want to learn how to hotwire a car?"

"What's that got to do with anything?" She asked as I pulled out of the hospital parking lot.

"It's one of my skills. If we're learning all of each other's skills, I'll teach you how to hotwire a car and how to set the ignition points in a classic Pontiac GTO."

"You haven't used either of those skills since we met. On the other hand, we have to write reports after every investigation."

"Just because I haven't used them recently, doesn't mean that they're not valuable skills in the right situation. I could give you a quick high speed driving tutorial while we're at it."

"That I might actually use."

"After that, I'll teach you how to eject a magazine and insert a new one without taking your aim off the target during a gunfight."

Jill sighed. "I suppose that's one of those skills you don't need often, but when you do, the need is urgent, and my life might depend on it."

"I knew a St. Paul PD range officer who could fire three magazines without missing a beat. And every shot was in the kill zone."

"He's the guy I'd like behind me in a gunfight."

I glanced at Jill. "Not necessarily. There are people who are great shots on the range but go to pieces and hide behind a car when the shooting starts. Personally, I'd rather have you backing me up more than any other cop I've ever met."

"You're bullshitting me."

"Nope. I know you'll be there when I need you, not hiding behind the nearest dumpster. If you fire your weapon, it's going to hit the target."

"Thank you."

I glanced at her. "And you're pretty good in bed."

"Damn it, Fletcher! Couldn't you just leave it be? You just have to kid around."

"You are pretty good in bed."

Jill snorted and faced the passenger window. "Only pretty good. I thought I was fabulous."

I started laughing, which garnered a look.

"The car wash is up ahead. Let's get out and I'll pay for the super deluxe wash, wax, and hand dry. We'll walk the line and find our hoodie guy, then confront him."

"Really? We're buying a deluxe wash for a rental pickup? Why don't we just ask about the guy, then confront him?"

"We're using subterfuge to lull him into a false sense of security by looking like customers rather than cops."

Jill looked at the lean young men wiping off a Cadillac as we drove past the car wash exit. "I don't know how we'll recognize him based on the grainy security pictures."

"Yeah. These guys all look like they just got out of jail. If we flash a badge, half of them will run."

"What will the other half do, assault us?"

"After six bags of drugs and two guns fall on the floor, I think they'll interlace their fingers behind their heads and face the wall with their feet spread apart."

"They'll drop their guns? Yeah, right, smartass."

"Having a firearm or drugs is a parole violation. If we can't identify who dropped what, we can't arrest anyone." As I walked to the cashier, I smiled and whispered, "In return for that knowledge, I expect you to write the hospital security letter."

"Fine. But don't expect me to include your name on it."

The cashier was the only woman working in the car wash and probably the only person the boss trusted to handle the money. Approaching her, I said, "We'll have the ultimate wash and dry."

She nodded, took my credit card, and rang up the sale. She appraised Jill and me as she waited for the credit card slip to print out. "Please don't terrorize my boys. I can't afford to have any of them run off."

Jill cocked her head. "Why would we…"

The cashier waved off Jill's question. "You two walk, talk, and smell like cops. Don't harass my boys."

Jill leaned close as we walked away from the cashier. "What do cops smell like?"

I made a show of making sure no one could hear us. I leaned close and said, "doughnuts."

"Cut that out!" she said before punching me in the arm. "Can't you be serious for fifteen minutes?"

"Do they have to be continuous, or can I spread my minutes out over the rest of the day?"

"I think I hear your mother calling. Yes, there it is. 'Doug, quit irritating your wife.'"

"Is that your best imitation of my mother's voice? That sounded like Barbara Streisand. My mother sounds more like Debbie Reynolds."

Jill spun around to face me. "The guys are staring at us. They know you're a cop."

"Walk into the office. It'll look like you're walking to the bathroom. Then, loop around the building and grab whoever runs out the other end of the car wash."

"What if more than one runs?" Jill asked as she stepped toward the office.

"Grab the biggest one."

She froze. "Why the biggest one?"

"Big guys don't usually hit women. You'll be saving me from a beating."

"Oh, great," Jill said as she walked away. "I get the big guy…again. Too bad my tough husband can't defend me from the big guy for a change…" Her rant continued as the office door closed behind her.

I walked down a customer aisle separated from the wash line by windows. As the cashier predicted, the guys looked at me like I was a cop. Most looked away. One big bruiser held eye contact with me as a challenge. I winked at him, which brought an expression of disgust. The first guy at the end of the line was wiping cars. Pencil thin with a wispy moustache, he reminded me of regular drug users I'd encountered. Something about the moustache caught my eye. Although the hospital security video was grainy and the hoodie hid its owner's upper face, the scraggly moustache and shape of his chin were distinctive.

The skinny guy locked eyes with me for a fraction of a second, then he dropped the towel he'd been using to wipe a Mercedes SUV. He'd taken two steps toward the road when he stumbled, lost his balance and fell. Jill was on his back, pulling his left arm as if she was going to handcuff him.

"I haven't done nothin'," he protested.

"I haven't done anything," I corrected.

"What?" the guy asked as Jill helped him to his feet.

"I corrected your grammar. The proper phrase is, 'I haven't done anything.'"

"Who are you, the English cops?"

"They're called Bobbies," I replied.

Looking confused he asked, "Who are called Bobbies?"

"English policemen are called Bobbies."

We continued the inane conversation as we guided the young man out of the building until we were standing by a dumpster, next to the neighboring business, out of earshot of the other car wash employees. "What's your name?"

"Who wants to know?"

I got into the guy's face. "I want to know what your name is."

"Why?"

"I think you're under a misconception about who asks the questions during a police interrogation."

"Call Steve Langevin. He'll vouch for me."

I sighed and looked at Jill. "The Hilo rumor mill must function on that 'hang loose' philosophy. This guy hasn't heard that Langevin's been arrested."

That white lie got the kid's attention. "Who arrested Langevin?"

"We're federal cops. We can take you over to Honolulu for further questioning. Or you can give us your side of the story about stealing the money, credit cards, and camera memory card from the Hilo morgue."

"I've got nothing to say."

"Fine. That makes you the fall guy. When Steve finds out that we've arrested you, he'll roll so fast it'll make your head spin."

"Listen, I did Steve a little favor, that's all. I gave him everything."

"There's an American Express card missing."

"That sonofabitch! He's setting me up."

"Where are the other credit cards, the cash, and the camera memory card?"

"What memory card?"

"It's a little square, flat piece of plastic." I held my fingers about a centimeter apart.

"That's a memory card? Huh. Steve said it was something to do with a cell phone."

"Where is that stuff?"

"Steve put it into the cup holder in his squad car. I don't know what happened to any of it after he dropped me off."

Jill looked skeptical. "He put it in his cruiser?"

"The cops here all own their cars. The county pays them mileage and insurance."

"Back to my original question: what's your name?"

"Tommy Bahama."

I spun the kid around and held one arm behind his back while I took out my handcuffs.

"Hey, man. Whatcha doing?"

"I'm arresting you for stealing evidence in a federal investigation." I clipped one handcuff on his left wrist. "You have the right to remain silent…"

"Whoa! You can't arrest me. I'll be killed when the prisoners find out I'm Steve's snitch."

I pulled his right hand behind his back and clipped on the other handcuff. "What's your name, smartass?"

The sound of the second handcuff ratcheting tight changed the kid's demeanor. "The guys call me Tommy Bahama because my dad was a laborer from Puerto Rico. My name is Hernandez. Tomas Hernandez."

"Your buddies must've slept through geography," I said, visualizing the location of Puerto Rico, nearly a thousand miles southeast of the Bahamas.

"None of them are math wizards," Tommy added.

Jill rolled her eyes and whispered, "He doesn't know the difference between geography and geometry. Don't mention geology."

"Where do you live, Tommy?"

"Rent's expensive here. I live in the back of a garage with Joe and Nahoa. It's over on Kehana street."

"Why would you be killed in jail?" Jill asked.

"Like I said, the guys think I'm a snitch because I talk to Steve."

"You *are* a snitch, Tommy. You're Steve's informant."

"I don't tell him anything. I mean, nothing important."

"You just committed a burglary for him," Jill said.

"He threatened to 'out' me to my crew."

"Cops don't identify their confidential informants to anyone, especially to the snitch's crew."

"Steve's pissed because he thinks I've been shorting him." As soon as the words were out of Tommy's mouth, he realized what he'd said. "Shorting him, you know, not giving him all I know about…"

"Shorting him usually means he's supposed to be getting a cut of something and means you're not passing on his full cut of the take."

"No. No. No. It's not like that…"

Jill nudged me and nodded toward the car wash where work had stopped. Seven guys were watching us. "We know where we can find Tommy. Let's release him," she whispered.

Panic swept Tommy's face. "You can't turn me loose," he hissed, breaking out in sweat.

"Why not?" Jill asked.

He nodded toward the car wash workers watching us. "My crew will think I told you something if you set me loose. Leave the cuffs on and take me away."

I grabbed Tommy's left bicep and pushed him roughly toward our pickup, which was dripping water at the car wash exit. "Let's go," I said loudly.

Jill fell in step beside me. "Are you trying to get us killed? There are seven guys staring daggers at us, and you're going to walk right through them?"

"Be loud and proud," I whispered. "Tuck in the front of your shirt so your badge and pistol are exposed. Put your hand on the butt of your Glock."

Taking the lead, Jill stepped in front of me. "Federal officers! Step back."

The crew looked unhappy, but they separated. I pushed Tommy ahead of me and Jill spun around, facing the car wash crew as she backed toward the pickup. I eased Tommy into the backseat, making sure he didn't bang his head on the door frame. With Tommy in the pickup, I got in on the driver's side and started the engine. Jill stood alongside the truck with her door open until I shifted the pickup into drive.

"Holy shit," she said as she slammed the door. "That was tense."

I cut her off by looking in the rear-view mirror, reminding her that we had a passenger.

She nodded, then looked at Tommy. "Turn around, Tommy, so I can take the cuffs off." With my handcuffs in her hand she asked, "Where would you like us to drop you off?"

"Behind the courthouse would be best. I can tell my boys that I'm out on bail."

"Why would they think we arrested you?" Jill asked, leaning over the seat to unlock the handcuffs on Tommy's wrists.

"I've got some quaaludes in my pocket. You should probably take them."

Jill looked at me. "He's got quaaludes in his pocket? Didn't you search his pockets before you put him into the pickup? You always tell me to pat people down when I cuff them."

I looked in the mirror. "Do you have a weapon?"

"Not on me," Tommy replied.

Jill turned and sat next to me, giving me the *you stupid idiot* look. At least that's the way I interpreted it. She'd never actually used those words.

"Did Steve tell you what to steal from the morgue?" I asked, looking at Tommy in the mirror.

"Nah. He thought there'd be a camera and maybe a video. All I found was that little chip, like it came from a phone. He was pissed that there wasn't a camera, but he seemed okay getting the chip." As an afterthought, Tommy added, "and the credit cards."

"You know that the credit cards have been reported as missing. If you use them, the cops will see your face on the store security cameras."

"They still work okay for internet purchases," Tommy replied.

Jill clenched her eyes shut, unable to believe any suspect was stupid enough to tell two cops he intended to use stolen credit cards for internet purchases. She twisted in her seat to face the back. "Tommy, are the credit cards in your pocket?"

"They're not on me."

"Where are they?"

Recognition swept Tommy's face. "Um…I sold them."

"You just admitted to stealing credit cards, then to selling them. Those are both felonies."

"I saw your badges. You're not real cops. You're just park rangers, like Steve."

"You're right," I said before Jill could reply. "We're just Park Service rangers. Tell us what Steve's getting cut short on."

"I can't. You guys will snitch and get him fired from his park gig."

"If it has nothing to do with the park, we're probably not interested," I replied, hoping to get Tommy to open up.

"Nope. Steve will get in trouble. Then he'll be all over my ass."

"As long as no one has died, it's probably not a big deal," Jill said, feeding Tommy some rope, and hoping he'd hang himself with it.

I was watching Tommy in the mirror, and when Jill said, "died," Tommy clenched his muscles. Tommy's eyes met mine, then he looked around at the residential neighborhood I was driving through. "You can let me out here. It's far enough from the car wash."

"Who died, Tommy?"

The rental pickup's rear doors weren't locked like they would've been in a police cruiser. Without warning, the rear passenger door flew open, and Tommy leaped out. I jammed on the brakes. Because I'd only been driving 20 mph, Tommy rolled once, then jumped to his feet. Before we were stopped, he'd disappeared between two houses.

Jill's door was open, and she was ready to pursue Tommy, but I stopped her. "Let him go. We can find him if we need him."

"But he knows more. He might know about the hiker deaths."

"I think he was done," I replied. "I doubt Steve told him about the hiker deaths. I think Tommy knows about a different crime."

Jill stepped back into the truck. "I'm sure he read about the hiker deaths in the paper."

"Think about that for a second. Does Tommy look like someone who reads a newspaper?"

"Maybe on the television news…" Jill stopped. "He probably doesn't watch the evening news either."

"Tommy either saw or heard about a different death."

Jill thought for a moment. "That's why Steve wanted the camera and memory card."

I made a U-turn. "We're going back to the park visitor center."

"Why?"

"Let's find out if the memory card is still in Steve's car."

"I shouldn't have to remind you that there's a law about having probable cause and a warrant before searching private property."

"There's an exclusion for evidence that's in plain sight."

"Okay. Tommy said that Steve put the memory chip in his car's cup holder. How is that in plain sight?"

"We're going to tell Steve that the pickup's tire has a slow leak. I'm driving it to the rental place to have it fixed. You're going to ask Steve for a ride to the B&B. Once he's invited you into the car, any evidence that's in plain sight, like in a cup holder, can be seized."

"I'm not comfortable with this," Jill replied as she shifted in her seat. "You want me to take the memory card out of Steve's cup holder while he's sitting next to me?"

I smiled. "You'll find a creative way to distract him so you can grab the chip. Use your feminine wiles."

"I don't see that form of distraction working well, dear."

Smiling at her I said, "I'm sure Mandy has offered hints on messing with a man's psyche. When you have the chip, hold it in your palm until you get a chance to put it in your pocket."

"You mean, palm it, like a magician hiding a coin."

"Exactly," I said.

"A magician practices that trick for weeks before performing it."

I took a dime out of my pocket. "Here you go. Practice."

I dropped the dime into the pickup's empty cup holder. Jill practiced picking it up. After several attempts, she held up her fist. She dropped the dime from her fist into her other hand. "The hardest part is getting the coin out of the cup holder. It's good that I had some practice with a coin before trying to pick up the memory card. It's harder than you'd guess."

Chapter 8

Steve Langevin was talking to a group of tourists inside the visitor center. Jill went to the restroom while I looked at one of the displays, killing time while waiting for Steve to finish. A couple minutes later, the tourists moved to the displays and Steve approached me. "I assume the pathologist told you that the hikers died from inhaling the volcanic laze."

"He also said they had broken legs and other injuries consistent with a fall."

"I'm sure they fell down before they died."

"They fell from a height. He'd only seen that type of injury in people who'd fallen from a waterfall or balcony. Not someone who had stumbled while hiking."

Staring toward the windows, Steve feigned indifference. "They died from inhaling the volcanic laze. That's the cause of death. Case closed."

Jill joined us, rubbing her hands as if they weren't quite dry. "Did you talk to Steve about your tire?"

"You have a tire problem?" Steve asked.

"The pickup has a slow leak. I'm going to the rental agency to see if they want to install the spare tire, or if they want me to take it to a shop to have it fixed. Could you give Jill a ride to the B&B?"

Jill sighed. "The only thing I hate more than sitting around a car repair shop is… Wow, I can't think of anything worse."

Looking annoyed, and checking his watch, Steve waffled for a moment. "It's close to quitting time. Where's your B&B?"

"In Volcano Village. Mary Johnson runs it."

"That's sort of on my way home. Give me two minutes to lock my office."

Jill held up crossed fingers as Steve walked away. "Let's hope this works."

* * *

When I arrived at the B&B after driving around for half an hour, Mary Johnson was straightening the magazines displayed on a coffee table in front of a rattan couch. The rest of the living room area had already been cleaned and arranged so it looked like no one had ever sat on a chair, perused a magazine, or stepped on the gleaming tile floor. She smiled and nodded toward the kitchen. "Jill's drinking iced tea on the patio. Would you like a glass, too?"

"Thanks, but no. We have some homework to take care of, then we'll go out for supper."

Hearing my voice, Jill joined us.

After a moment of thought, Mary's eyes lit up. "You should try the Slippery Squid, down by the harbor. The atmosphere is nothing to write home about, but their seafood is fresh and well prepared. Be sure to ask about the day's fresh catch."

Jill looked skeptical. "I saw their sign when we drove through town. It reminded me of the bars my dad took us to for hamburgers when I was a kid. They were loud, smoky, and full of sweaty drunken cowboys."

Mary nodded. "Move that ambiance to Hilo. Substitute fishermen for the cowboys and remember that Hawaii is smoke-free." She paused. "I bet the burgers were great at the spots your dad chose."

"They were, once you got past smoke, sweat, and rowdy cowboys."

Mary's eyes gleamed. "If mahi mahi is on the chalkboard, order it. You'll never have better fish."

"I suppose the owner makes up for the lack of ambiance with good food and reasonable prices," I said.

"The lack of ambiance *is* the ambiance. The weathered sign and siding are meant to attract tourists who want a *real* Hawaii experience. The fishermen get their first beer free, so there's always a local vibe."

Jill looked at me. "It sounds like Fin's Grill in Port Aransas. I think that sounds like fun. I'd like to clean up and put on a fresh shirt before we go."

Once out of Mary's sight, I asked Jill, "How did your sleight of hand go?"

She took the memory chip out of her pocket and held it up. "I didn't need my magician skills. A BMW blew past us as we pulled out of the visitor center parking lot. Steve pulled him over and ticketed him for speeding. I was alone in the car for four or five minutes while Steve dealt with the driver. The memory chip was in the cup holder."

"Easy."

"Yeah. Sure. I had to dig through all the crap Steve had jammed into his cup holder while watching him talk with the speeder. I'm not cut out to be a thief. My hands were shaking, and I was sweating the whole time. When Steve came back to the car, he looked at me like he knew what I'd done."

"Did he confront you?"

"No, he asked if I was sick. He said I was shaking and sweaty. I told him I might be coming down with something."

"Good reply. I'm surprised Steve hadn't disposed of the memory card."

"Don't be surprised. The inside of Steve's car resembles his office. The memory chip was in the cup holder with gum wrappers, paper napkins, and used toothpicks. If not for the speeder, I would've struggled to free it from the crap jammed alongside it."

"Dr. Nakamura recorded the card's serial number on the inventory," I said.

Jill held up the card and turned it, trying to find the serial number. "There are some tiny numbers on the back side. The font is too small for me to read. Maybe you'll be able to see it using your Sherlock Holmes magnifying glass."

"Gee, I left that at home with my cape, deerstalker cap, and pipe."

"As I recall, Sherlock injected a 7% cocaine solution to heighten his perception and reasoning skills."

"Ah, that explains why my arrest and conviction rates were never 100%, like Sherlock's."

Jill chuckled. "As I recall, Sherlock never married. And here you are, partnered with a smart, witty wife. I'm sure your arrest and conviction rates will skyrocket."

"You left out the part about you being humble."

Jill looped her arm into mine. "My humility goes without saying."

* * *

Inside our room, Jill took the chip to the bathroom. "What are you up to?" I asked.

"There's a magnifying mirror on the counter. I used it when I plucked my eyebrows."

"You pluck your eyebrows?"

"You're so clueless." After a moment Jill said, "Write down this number."

With the serial number written on the pad next to the phone, I punched in Dr. Nakamura's office phone number and left a message asking him to reply with the serial number of the missing memory card. Then I took out my laptop computer, hoping the dime-sized memory card would fit into the tiny slot I'd never had a reason to use on the side.

Jill closed the blinds. The laptop warmup seemed to take forever. "Would you care to wager about what's on the memory card?" I asked.

"The loser buys supper," Jill suggested as the home screen loaded. "I bet there are wedding pictures."

Scoffing, I shook my head. "Really? You think there are wedding pictures on the memory card?"

"I figure this memory card can probably hold a thousand pictures. Every photographer has worked a wedding."

"There's got to be something Steve doesn't want people to see—something that implicates him in a crime."

Jill slipped the card into the slot and pulled the computer onto her lap. "What cop is going to let a photographer take pictures of a drug deal? It's probably Steve acting stupid at a bachelor party."

"Maybe the photographer was working undercover for the Kona police and caught Steve doing something."

"Interesting. Maybe the photographer got pictures of Steve sneaking a woman other than his wife into a motel room. Or getting naked under a waterfall."

Sensing a memory card in the slot, the photo program opened automatically, displaying a hundred icons. Each file appeared to be one photo session. "Wow. This must represent several months worth of work," I said. "Open the most recent file."

"It's full of flowers," Jill said, looking at the thumbnail pictures. "Here's a picture of the Hawaii Arboretum sign."

"What's the file before the arboretum?"

Jill closed the flower pictures and opened the next file. "Whale watching pictures, like the ones you'd see in a travelogue. Most are splashes and tails, but here's one of a breaching humpback whale." She clicked on the thumbnail to enlarge it. "Wow, that's spectacular."

"There was an .mpg file earlier. Open it."

It took longer for the movie file to open. Jill leaned close to the screen to see the images. "It's ambient light movies of a night pool party. It looks like someone's birthday."

I watched, focusing on a couple standing on the far side of the pool. "It's not a birthday party. Look at this couple. They're way too cozy to be at a birthday party."

"Oh gawd," Jill said. "It makes my skin crawl just watching that guy rubbing the girl's arm. I think she's drunk, and he's trying to talk her into going somewhere more private."

The image blurred as the photographer swung the camera quickly to the side. He stopped when he got to two men throwing punches. "Those guys are seriously mad," I said. "I think the blonde guy's already missing a couple of teeth."

Jill clucked her tongue. "They're going to regret this night when they sober up."

A man rushed forward and stepped between the two combatants, pushing them apart. "I think that's Steve Langevin," I said.

"Yeah, it is Steve, wearing sandals, shorts, and a Hawaiian shirt. He looks sober."

The fighters were pushed apart. People moved the combatants to chairs and inspected their injuries. Then the movie jumped to a new scene of people standing around a tiki bar situated next to the pool. "Back that up," I said, pointing to the image of Steve on the left edge of the screen.

"What did you see?" Jill asked as she moved the time slider back to an earlier point in the video.

"I think Steve passed a guy some drugs. Watch his hand." A shirtless man in surfer shorts walked up to Steve and leaned close. "Watch Steve's hand."

After a brief verbal exchange, Steve reached into his pocket, then held his hand next to his leg. The surfer touched Steve's hand, exchanging money for a small packet. "I would've missed it if you hadn't pointed it out," Jill said.

"It's like a magic trick. It's meant to not be seen. If you're not watching their hands, it's easy to be distracted by them smiling and talking. Drug dealers master that skill so they can exchange drugs for money in the open."

"Steve must've wanted this video of his drug dealing activity," Jill said. "Is this enough to arrest him?"

"It'd be enough to get a search warrant for his house and car. We'd need the drugs to get a conviction."

Jill was getting into the video. She leaned closer to the screen to see it better. "Let's keep watching. Maybe there's something more overt."

I leaned back. "We're only three minutes into an hour-long video. Let's eat supper and come back to this later."

"I'm not really hungry," Jill replied, paging through other thumbnail file images on the screen.

"The video will still be here later. Actually, it might be better if we watched it when we're fresh."

We were walking to the pickup when my phone buzzed. The caller ID showed the pathologist's number. "You got my message?"

Nakamura sounded excited. "Did you recover the memory card?"

"I have a Sandisk memory card. If you read me the serial number from the inventory of the victim's belongings, I'll tell you if I have the missing card."

I smiled at Jill as I matched the number she'd read to me with the number being relayed by the pathologist. "Thanks, Doc. We've got the missing memory card."

"Do you know if it contains something criminal?"

"I can't comment."

"Yeah, yeah. The investigation is ongoing."

I chuckled. "I'll let you know what's on it when I can share the information."

"Fletcher?"

"Yeah."

"An inspector from the Hawaiian Office of Healthcare Compliance showed up today. The CEO and legal counsel spent the day touring them through the facility and reviewing our safety and security protocols. There was a hospital board meeting this morning. A source told me that the board approved a million-dollar upgrade to our security systems and training."

"Excellent!"

Jill looked at me expectantly. "What was that about?"

"A state inspector showed up at the hospital and they're going to spend a million dollars to upgrade their security."

After considering that for a moment, Jill said, "Nakamura assumes that we're the ones who reported them."

"He didn't speculate on that, but I'm sure we're persona non grata in the hospital. I hope we don't need emergency care before the end of this assignment."

"I think the doctors and nurses will be delighted that we precipitated an improvement in security. On the other hand, I don't want to bump into the CEO if we're being treated in the ER."

"Were you planning on visiting the ER?" I asked.

"Doug, somehow your plans don't coincide with the final outcome of most investigations."

* * *

As expected, the Slippery Squid had the ambiance of a Texas shrimp shack. The walls were decorated with fishing nets, glass floats, stuffed sharks, and beer signs. The bar running along the far wall was lined with men whose arms were tattooed, deeply tanned, and well muscled, all in workmen's clothing. About half of them appeared to have significant native Hawaiian heritage, the others were a mix of Asians, Whites, and Blacks.

The restaurant part of the building was half full. A sign directed us to seat ourselves.

After delivering meals to a neighboring table, an attractive woman turned to us. "Do you want menus, or are you just here for happy hour?"

"We'd like menus please," I said.

Checking a clock over the bar, the waitress handed us menus and said, "It's happy hour for another ten minutes. Draft beer and rail drinks are $1 off."

I ordered a local draft beer while Jill studied a chalkboard next to the bar. When a waitress walked past with a round of drinks that looked like whipped cream floating on water, Jill asked our waitress, "What are those?"

"It's our signature drink. Baileys Irish Cream floated on Sambuca topped with whipped cream and a cherry. It's called a Slippery Nipple."

Jill's intrigue evaporated. "I'll have a mai tai."

"Good choice. The bartender uses fresh squeezed juices and local rum."

I leaned close after the waitress left with our drink orders. "Sambuca and Baileys sound really good together."

"I don't like licorice flavored anything and I'm not drinking something called a slippery nipple."

I listened to the light conversations around us while we waited for our drinks. Laughter erupted from the bar area, and overall, the restaurant was cheerful and pleasant. Jill put her hand on mine. "Earth calling Doug."

"Sorry. I was enjoying the surroundings."

"We've been in so many bars where I felt like I had to watch my back, that this seems oddly at ease."

"I guess that Hawaiian 'hang loose' motto is deserved."

Our waitress set my beer and Jill's drink, garnished with a pineapple wedge and a tiny umbrella, on coasters and pulled out an order pad. "Tonight's fresh catch is hebi. It's a short-billed swordfish that's grilled, then dressed with shallots and drizzled with white wine sauce." She leaned over and wiped up a spot of condensation from my beer glass and whispered. "If you like salt-water fish, hebi is great. This preparation is wonderful. I think the kitchen is almost out of it, but I can rush your order back."

I smiled and handed my menu to the waitress. "You sold me on the hebi." Jill nodded.

I glanced at the waitress as she hustled our order to the kitchen. "She didn't mention the price."

Jill lifted her glass and touched it to the rim of my beer mug. "A toast to the unknown. To a variety of fish we've never eaten before at a price that may exceed our per diem."

I started to laugh.

"What's so funny?"

"I had a partner when I was in uniform. The only place he'd eat was a burger joint with a castle logo. The burgers were called sliders and they were the cheapest meal at any fast-food place."

"He ate there because it was cheap?"

"Yeah, old Charlie had been divorced three times and could barely afford to buy gas for his commute to the station. He'd tell me to order for him, then he'd slip off to the bathroom, so I had to pay."

"He was doing you a favor by keeping the price down."

"I would've bitched if we'd been ordering steak, but when we were eating $3 burger baskets, it wasn't a big deal. Besides, I felt sorry for the poor guy. That, and he was the second-best partner I ever had. We worked the graveyard shift, and he had the eyes of a hawk. We'd pass closed businesses and he'd watch for a silhouette against the night lights inside the stores. We'd make a burglary arrest every week because Charlie would spot someone where they shouldn't be."

"You said he was your second-best partner. Who was your best?"

"I'm having supper with her."

"Fletcher, you are so full of shit…" Jill sampled her mai tai and smiled. "My god, this is heavenly. The waitress was right about the fresh squeezed fruit. I've never had a drink as good as this."

The waitress delivered our plates as Jill swilled down half her mai tai. "Ignore the argument in the kitchen," she said, looking over her shoulder. "The other waitress thought there were two more servings of hebi left. The cook just told her they were gone as I carried your dinners past her."

A different waitress was berating someone in the kitchen. Our waitress' eyes sparkled. "Don't feel bad. She did it to me last night with the mahi mahi special."

Jill's dimples appeared and she shook her head. "If this meal is as good as it smells, you may have earned yourself a nice tip."

"Ma'am, if this isn't the best hebi you've ever eaten, it's on the house."

"That's a safe bet since we're from South Dakota and Minnesota and have never had hebi before." Jill finished her mai tai and held up her empty glass. "I'd like another mai tai, please."

"We don't get a lot of midwestern folks in Hilo. For some reason, they think Maui is the place to take vacations. Personally, I can't stand the traffic there, and the prices are insane. I much prefer Hilo to even the Kona side of this island. Hilo is more Hawaiian, and the pace is slower with fewer tourists around."

"The guys at the bar seem pretty mellow."

"They're our regulars. They're the hardworking folks who make everything function. They're cowboys, fishermen, electricians, a plumber, and a carpenter. The bartender treats them well because they kept us afloat during the Covid shutdown. You wouldn't believe how many places went out of business when the governor enacted the ten-day quarantine for all arriving tourists."

I unfolded the paper napkin wrapping our silverware as the waitress walked away. Jill inhaled the aroma as she picked up her fork. "If this is as good as it smells, we might eat here every night for the rest of our Hilo stay."

"Just don't ask for a *big* glass of wine like you did in Miami."

"I'd forgotten about that. The waitress brought me the piano player's tip jar. It must've held an entire bottle of wine." Sadness swept Jill's face. "I hope that waitress got her life sorted out."

I thought about the friendship we'd developed with the young waitress over a few nights, only to be swept into her life crisis and eventually stepping in and delivering her to the hospital after her boyfriend assaulted her. "Let's stay on a first-name basis with this waitress…"

Reading my thoughts, Jill nodded. Savoring her first bite of hebi, Jill closed her eyes.

"It's that good?" I asked as I stabbed a bite of the fish with my fork.

"I can't believe the mahi mahi can possibly be better than this." Turning toward the bar, Jill signaled our waitress.

"How's the hebi?" the waitress asked.

"It's great, but a mai tai isn't the right drink."

Nodding, the waitress said, "The chef uses Pinot Grigio in the sauce. Would you like a glass of that instead of a second mai tai?"

"Yes, please."

"Wine for you, sir?"

"I'll take another Kona Longboard."

The waitress paused. "You two are cops, right?"

"Off duty cops," I replied.

Jill swallowed and looked at the waitress. "We're not wearing badges or guns. How did you make us as cops?"

"Mary called from the B&B to make sure we were treating her cops well. You're a little less shaggy than the locals, and less wrinkled than the tourists."

"Do cops have a *look*?" I asked.

She looked at me. "Your haircut is shorter and fresher than average. You glance at the door every time it opens, like you're expecting a robber to walk in. And you're not swilling foo-foo drinks with umbrellas like you're trying to forget your stressful mainland jobs." She looked at Jill. "You look less like a cop than he does. I'll get your wine."

"I'm not sure if looking less like a cop is a compliment."

"Trust me, it is."

The waitress sped back with Jill's wine in a frosty glass. She turned away, then smiled and spoke to Jill. "You look too classy to be a cop." Then she rushed off.

"There you go!" I said, "You look too classy to be a cop."

"You're making fun of me."

"I've always said you look classy."

"If you're trying to talk me into romance."

"I tell other people that you're classy, too."

"Who?"

"Um…Matt."

"Who else?"

I must've blinked a couple times while my mind raced. "I told Jack you were classy."

"You tell our bosses that I'm classy."

Remembering Jill's advice to stop digging when I hit the bottom of the hole, I shut up.

"What flavor is your shoe?"

"I must've stepped in some spilled beer when I walked in."

Letting me off the hook, Jill nodded at something behind me. "I think the Don of Hilo is holding court behind you. I swear that everyone in the dining room has gone to his table to kiss his ring."

To get a better look, I bent down and straightened my pants cuff. The man was large, with Hawaiian facial features. The men sitting on either side of him looked like bodyguards, and the blonde across from him was trying for a Hollywood starlet look.

"Yes, he looks like a mafioso."

"I wonder if the woman with him is a hooker or his daughter."

"I'm guessing she's his administrative assistant."

Jill snorted. "An admin wearing a white miniskirt and four-inch heels. Get real."

When the waitress brought my beer and Jill's second glass of wine, I whispered, "Who's the guy with the bodyguards?"

"That's Jake Kahana."

"Is he with the local mafia?"

Our waitress giggled. "He sells real estate. The guys with him are his sons and the woman is the oldest son's wife."

"Not mafia," I said.

"Close," the waitress said. "He's working on a deal to build a timeshare development next to Volcano Village."

"Is it happening soon?"

"I doubt people are that stupid. The last lava flow covered a quarter of the land he'd bought for the golf course. The rumor is that they're trying to figure out how they can interest people in a resort with an 11-hole golf course."

We were down to the last bites of our fish when the waitress checked on us. "Can I interest you in dessert?"

I shook my head. "I've got no room."

The waitress looked at Jill. "I overheard you say you didn't want a Slippery Nipple because you weren't into Sambuca. We make a Jellyfish Shot that's Baileys floated on Amaretto and crème de cacao. The Baileys floats on top of the clear liquor, so it looks like a jellyfish."

The panic in Jill's eyes made me laugh. "I think we'll just have our bill."

Leaning across the table, Jill whispered, "I think the jellyfish thing would gag me. I'm not drinking or eating anything that looks like a jellyfish."

Our bill arrived and I was surprised to see a ten percent discount. I flagged the waitress. "We can't accept a cop discount."

"That's not because you're cops. The B&B guests all get a discount. Mary sends us a lot of business."

Jill snatched the bill out of my hand and held out her credit card.

"What are you up to?" I asked.

"You're not noted for your generosity when it comes to tips. I'm paying so I can tip an amount commensurate with the level of service we received."

"What would that percentage be?"

The conversation ended when the waitress delivered the folio with the credit card slip and Jill's card. She held the pen over the tip line while doing math, then she wrote down a figure, totaled the sum, and signed the slip.

"That's fifty percent!" I said, expecting her to correct the amount.

She tucked the credit card in her back pocket, stood, and smiled. "If not for her, we wouldn't have had hebi."

I stood and pulled Jill close before kissing the top of her head. "That may be her biggest tip of the night."

"I hope so. And I hope she serves us again when we come back tomorrow night."

* * *

Mary Johnson was nowhere in sight when we returned to the B&B. We let ourselves into our room. Jill closed the door and leaned against it, obviously feeling the effects of the wine on top of the mai tai. "I'm not ready to watch the rest of the video. Let's leave it for tomorrow."

"I'm fine with that plan. Nothing is going to change between now and morning."

Jill walked to the bathroom with purpose, then closed the door.

"Are you okay?" I asked through the door.

"Mai tais, wine, and fish with wine sauce might not be a good mixture."

"I think the problem might be the volume of alcohol more than the mixture."

Chapter 9

After sipping a cup of tea in the breakfast nook, Jill scooped out tiny bits of the half papaya Mary served us. The aroma of fresh muffins wafted out of the kitchen. "Mmm," I said to Jill. "I can almost taste the muffins. I wonder if Mary puts macadamia nuts in them?"

Jill glanced at the kitchen door. "I can still taste last night's fish. It wasn't that long ago that it made a return trip."

Mary carried in plates with two muffins on each. "Pineapple and macadamia nut muffins this morning." She looked at the tentative scoops of papaya Jill had sampled. "Tummy's not happy this morning?"

"The hebi, mai tais, and white wine didn't mix well. I'm sure I'll perk up in a couple of hours."

"I'll put your muffins in a bag. You can eat them later." Turning to me, halfway through the first muffin, Mary asked, "Would you like a couple eggs and some bacon?"

Jill clenched her eyes shut and took deep breaths while apparently suppressing her gag reflex. "I'll stick with the papaya and muffins this morning."

"You need a little protein to carry you until lunch."

"How about a couple cups of coffee to go?"

Mary smiled. "No problem."

Jill looked up. "Make mine tea, please."

"Sure. Tea, coffee, and two muffins to go."

"We can go back to the room and watch the rest of the video on the memory card," I suggested as Mary carried Jill's muffins away.

"No."

"But..."

"Doug, watching moving images on the computer screen would be a bad idea right now."

"Are you up to riding around in the car?"

Jill hung her head. "If you don't make any quick turns, and don't drive down any streets with speed bumps I should be able to handle a car ride."

"I've got Dramamine in my shaving kit. Would you like me to bring you a couple of them?"

"They put me to sleep." Jill paused, then added, "What the hell. Asleep is probably better than throwing up into the truck's footwell."

"I'm sure that throwing up inside the truck would invoke the extra cleaning charges."

"Paying a cleaning charge is not..." Jill turned grayer, then hustled toward our room before finishing the sentence.

Mary returned with a white bakery bag and two Styrofoam cups. "What happened to Jill?"

"She went to get Dramamine from our room."

Mary sat in the chair opposite me. "Is she going to be okay? I'm sure I could get a clinic appointment for her."

"I think the mai tai was a bit stronger than she realized."

"They slide down like soda pop," Mary said with a knowing smile. "You sometimes pay for your overindulgence the next day."

Mary and I chatted about life in Hilo while we waited for Jill to return. Looking ashen and tired, Jill sat next to me. "Let's stay here a while. I'll have some more tea while I sit in the room. You can call Jack to update him on our progress."

Mary stood, not wanting to intrude on our discussion.

"How bad do you feel?" I whispered.

"I think it'd be wise to sip tea near the bathroom for a while."

I took my cup of coffee to the patio and settled into a rattan chair overlooking a small pool. Bougainvillea petals dropped onto the water from a nearby bush that appeared to be a hedge between the B&B and the neighboring house. Punching Jack's number into the phone, I leaned back and thought about the unwatched video on the memory card.

"Hi Doug, I was wondering when I'd get an update from you."

"As I recall, you thought something was amiss when you read Steve Langevin's report on the dead hikers."

"I'm not sure amiss is the right word. His report seemed incomplete. Have you been able to fill in any of the holes?"

I explained our brief opening discussion with the superintendent and Langevin, then recapped our experience at the hospital and the car wash. "The good news is we recovered the memory chip that was missing from the morgue."

"You're sure it's the correct chip?"

"We checked the serial numbers with the pathologist last night. It's the chip stolen from the morgue."

"Where did you find it?"

"In the cup holder inside Steve Langevin's police car."

"You got a search warrant for his car?"

"No. He gave Jill a ride to our B&B, and the chip was in plain sight sitting inside a cup holder."

"He let her take the chip?"

I sighed. "Langevin doesn't know it's missing. Jill removed it while he was out of the car."

"Does that make anything you discover fruit from the poisonous tree that's inadmissible in court?"

"The 'plain view' doctrine says an officer can seize evidence he can see inside a vehicle or even a house if it's not hidden from view. Langevin invited Jill into his car and the memory chip was sitting in the open. Hell, it might've even been visible through his windshield, so we could've opened the car door and seized it that way."

"You suspect there's something incriminating in the pictures on the chip?"

"I don't know why else Langevin would risk stealing it from the morgue. We looked at a few images last night. Most of the photo files were the victim's work, pictures he'd taken for his employer. We also found one video of a party with one suspicious scene that looks like Langevin making a drug deal."

"Keep me posted."

I'd just ended the call when Mary brought a coffee carafe to the patio. "If you're going to work out here, you might as well drink coffee."

"Thank you."

"Are you going to check on Jill?"

"She was having stomach cramps and I didn't want to…"

Mary nodded. "Let me know if either of you need anything."

I'd just closed my eyes and leaned back in the lounge chair, feeling the sun warm my face when the chair next to me creaked and an unfamiliar woman's voice asked, "Are you some kind of cop?"

The young woman sitting next to me was dressed in a skimpy fuchsia bikini. A sheen of sweat glistened on her skin suggesting she'd been sunning herself for a while. "Are you a guest here, too?" I asked, avoiding the woman's question.

She shook her head. "I live next door. I'm Mocha."

The woman's skin was creamy brown, the color of a Starbucks mocha coffee. "I'm Doug." Kicking myself for not being more situationally aware and letting someone unknown slip into a chair beside me, I smiled. "What makes you think I'm a cop?"

The woman glanced at my waist. "Even though you're in casual clothes, the badge on your belt is kind of a giveaway."

"I work for the National Park Service."

"That's not a ranger's badge."

"I'm a Park Service investigator."

The woman turned and leaned back in the lounge chair. "You look like a cop."

"What do cops look like?"

"You've usually got nicely trimmed hair, polished shoes, neat clothes without stains or holes."

"What makes you an expert on how cops look?"

"I've worked in enough strip clubs to recognize a cop when I see one. The boss usually warns us about the local regulations. When there's a cop in the audience, we limit the show to what's legal."

"Have you ever been wrong?"

Mocha chuckled. "If you're asking if I've got an arrest record, the answer is, yes."

"Most people with police records avoid cops."

"Most cops are nice enough away from the job. I've never had a cop rough me up or steal my tips."

"Good to know. Two points for good cops."

I expected Mocha to leave, but she remained in the chair. "I overheard you mention Steve Langevin."

Wondering how much of my phone conversation Mocha had overheard through the hedge, I asked, "Is Steve a friend of yours?"

"Steve's an arrogant prick who shouldn't be a cop."

"Ah, he's the exception to cops being okay people," I said.

"I have a problem."

Uh oh, I thought. "I can't fix parking tickets or erase convictions from your record."

Mocha giggled. "That was good." Turning serious she said, "I need to get off the island."

"You're broke and can't afford a plane ticket?"

"That too. My problem is more…situational."

"Do you have a degree in English?"

"What? Strippers aren't supposed to have a large vocabulary?"

"With a few exceptions, most of the strippers I've met weren't college graduates. On the other hand, some of the high-end call girls I've arrested had advanced college degrees."

Mocha was silent for a moment. "I got myself into a situation and I'm looking for a way out. I thought you might be able to help me find an option."

"If you're asking if I'll loan you money, the answer is no. If you're offering your personal services in exchange for whatever, the answer is still no. If you're asking if me, as a cop, can help you break away from something unsavory or illegal, the answer might be yes."

"You're a Park Service cop. Don't you feds talk with each other?"

"I investigate crimes inside park service properties. I have some contact with other federal agencies, but not every day. What do you need?"

"Did you notice my boobs?"

"Like I said, if we're talking about me as a person…"

"A drug dealer paid for my boob job. Now he thinks he owns me." When I didn't immediately respond, Mocha went on, "I'm stuck working in this strip club near the Hilo airport. The drug dealer and

Steve Langevin set me up as the owner on the club's liquor license, but they control what happens. They're using the club to launder money and they expect the dancers to be the entertainment at their private parties."

"In a perfect world, what would you like me to do?"

"I'd like you to discreetly bring someone here who can get me the hell out of this mess and back to the mainland without me being beaten, tortured, or killed. Can you do that, Doug?"

I heard women's laughter from the other side of the bougainvillea. "Do the other girls living with you feel the same?"

"They don't know I'm talking to a cop, if that's what you're asking."

"Do they want to leave Hawaii and return to the mainland?"

"They all want out of the business. I'm not sure what their plans are."

"Why don't all of you just leave?"

"Have you seen a bus station here, Doug? It's hard to break away from a pimp when you're in Chicago or Las Vegas. At least there you can hitchhike or catch a bus out of state. Hawaii seems like paradise, but there's an aspect that's hell, too. Once you're here, you have to take a plane or boat to leave."

"I know we just met, and this sounds like the oldest line in the book, but I need you to trust me. Stay here for two minutes while I get my partner."

Mocha leaned forward. "I'm sorry I bothered you. Just forget I was here."

I was tempted to touch her arm, but I was afraid she'd been grabbed by too many men, too many times. "My partner's name is Jill. She's a great sounding board and she's helped a couple of working girls get out of the business. Will you trust me for two minutes?"

"If your butt isn't back in that chair two minutes from now, I'll be gone. Don't bother knocking on the door. No one will be home."

* * *

Jill's color was returning, but she barely opened one eye when I walked into the room. She was lying on the bed with a forearm across her forehead.

"There's a woman by the pool who needs to speak with you."

"Tell her to come back tomorrow."

I extended my hand. "This is a 911 situation. Put on your game face and come with me."

"Let me splash some water on my face. I'll be out in a minute."

"Listen to me. There's an exploited woman out there who's ready to bolt. She gave me two minutes to bring you to the pool. I need you to hear her story."

Jill stood, then wobbled. "Whoa. That was bad."

I picked up Jill's badge and Glock, then pulled open the bedroom door. "Take my hand."

Mocha's sheen had turned into dripping sweat as she paced alongside the pool. Mary looked at me as we approached the pool. "I don't appreciate having *those women* over here."

"Trust me, it's not what you think."

I held the patio door open as Jill passed, then I looked at Mary, who was staring at me with her hands on her hips. "Could we get another coffee cup and some tea?"

"I don't…"

"This is police business. Please."

Mary turned.

Jill's hands were jammed in her pockets as she and Mocha spoke alongside the pool while I lingered inside the door. The longer they spoke, the less agitated Mocha became. Jill gestured towards four chairs set up around a patio table just as Mary came out of the kitchen carrying two pots, three cups, a porcelain container of tea bags, and a plate of scones on a platter. I opened the door for her.

"I heard there was a coffee and tea emergency out here," Mary said, setting the platter on the table. She smiled at Mocha and Jill before returning to the house.

Mocha sat at the table. "Doug says you've got experience with working girls."

Jill put two tea bags into the teapot while I poured coffee. "We were involved in an incident in South Dakota a year ago. As a matter of fact, Doug was nearly killed by a biker while saving a girl who was working out of a motel room."

Jill surveyed Mocha's tiny bikini and over-sized breasts. "A bikini like that wouldn't work for me."

Jill's comment broke the ice, and Mocha laughed. "It takes more than you've got to fill out a bikini top like this."

Realizing that my role had become superfluous. I let the women talk without interrupting.

"Doug only told me that you needed help. How can we assist you?"

"It all started with this damned boob job." Mocha explained all she'd told me, then, expanded on her thoughts as Jill asked questions and offered supportive comments.

Forty-five minutes later, with all the scones, coffee, and tea gone, Jill leaned back and looked at me. "What's the plan, Doug?"

"I don't have a plan. My whole plan was getting you out here to meet Mocha and hear her story."

Mocha leaned forward. "My professional name is Mocha. I'm Jocelyn Taylor, from Joliet, Illinois."

Jill extended her hand. "I'm Jill Fletcher, from Spearfish, South Dakota. My partner is Doug Fletcher, from St. Paul, Minnesota."

Mocha's rock-hard persona cracked, and tears filled her eyes. "I've got to get out of here before I'm killed."

"Can you hang on for a couple days while we make some contacts, or do you need to leave immediately?" Jill asked.

"Things are going south with Gil. He's getting flakier by the day, and I never know if the smooth, under control Gil is going to show up, or if it'll be the edgy scary guy who looks like he'd kill me if I said no to whatever crazy scheme he's throwing out."

"Is Gil the person you work for?"

Mocha nodded. "He financed the club and uses it to launder money."

"What's Gil's last name?"

"Jackson. Gil Jackson. He's also laundering money through his helicopter charter business."

Mocha looked around nervously. "I've got to go before the other girls get too suspicious. Make some noise late tomorrow morning when you're by the pool and I'll walk over."

"Are you sure you're safe until then?" Jill asked, placing her hand on Mocha's arm.

"Jill, you've provided me with a light at the end of the tunnel. I'll be able to get through whatever shit comes up for a day or two."

Mocha disappeared around the bougainvillea and Jill fell back into her chair like the air had been let out of her. "How long had you two been talking before you got me?"

"Maybe five minutes."

"How old do you think Mocha is?" Jill whispered.

I stared at the spot where Mocha had disappeared behind the hedge. "Maybe thirty-five? What's your guess?"

Jill looked at the spot where Mocha had gone out of sight as she considered the question, then shook her head. "I think she's barely out of college. She's seen and experienced too much in her few adult years."

I leaned close to Jill's ear. "Did you notice that she wore sandals with closed toes?"

"So?"

"If she's a user, she's probably hiding needle tracks between her toes."

"OMG!"

"Shh." I stood and gathered the cups and wiped up crumbs with a napkin.

"What are we going to do?"

"Find a phone number for the US Attorney in Honolulu. I need to kick this up the ladder. We're way over our heads and out of our jurisdiction."

Jill edged me away from the table and put her arms around my neck. "We're going to help her."

"Of course, we are. I'm going to call…"

"Doug, *WE are* going to help her."

"She needs someone from the DEA and maybe the Internal Revenue Service, not park rangers who are supposed to be investigating two suspicious deaths."

"You don't seem to understand, dear. She doesn't need a bunch of bureaucrats and lawyers. She needs two human beings; you and me."

"We have two deaths to investigate, dear."

"Don't call the US Attorney right away. We'll multi-task."

"We're already up to our…"

Jill put her fingers to my lips. "I give you permission to say, 'yes, dear' in this situation."

I closed my eyes for a moment, then smiled. "Yes, dear."

* * *

After bypassing the ranger at the welcome desk who was surrounded by a group of tourists, we found a ranger who'd just finished speaking with a middle-aged couple. She glanced at our badges and guns, immediately tensing. Jill's smile disarmed her.

"I'm Jill Fletcher and this is my partner, Doug. We're investigating the death of the people who were found on the lava flow."

"Oh man, that was terrible. I mean, why would they walk past the barriers and into the laze cloud. That's just..." She hesitated as a group of teenagers walked past.

"What's your name?" Jill asked.

"Tonya, Tonya Jackson."

"Were you working the day they were found?" I asked.

Tonya sighed. "Zoey and I opened the gate and drove to the ranger hut next to the lava. The first visitors reported the...find...to us. We walked out to check. It was...bad."

Jill nodded her understanding. "Did you notice any of their gear around the bodies?"

"Gear?"

"Did they have backpacks, water bottles, cell phones, or cameras?"

"Um, I don't recall anything but the bodies. And they were barely recognizable as bodies. If not for their shoes and the canvas vest the woman was wearing, I'm not sure I'd have recognized them as human."

"Did it seem odd that there wasn't any gear with them?" I asked.

"Odd how?"

"If they'd walked down from the gate, wouldn't you expect to find water bottles and maybe backpacks?" I asked.

"I guess that didn't occur to me. I was freaked out by realizing the bodies were there."

"Did you stay with the bodies until the Park Service team removed them?" Jill asked.

"Yeah. I had to turn away the tourists who were arriving. I couldn't let anyone onto the lava flow."

"Who recovered the bodies?"

"Gordo and Rascal are our rescue guys. It took them almost an hour to get to the lava flow with their gear. It was like half an hour after that until the ambulance from Volcano Village got here to take the bodies away."

Tonya became visibly shaken as we spoke. Jill put her hand on Tonya's arm. That gesture allowed Tonya to release the tension, bringing on sobs. I turned away while Jill pulled Tonya to her shoulder. Walking to the pickup, I considered Tonya's comments.

Jill met me at the pickup. "Tonya doesn't remember seeing any equipment or personal items with the bodies."

"That isn't uncommon for someone's first encounter with dead bodies. I was called to an empty lot on St. Paul's west side to investigate the report of a dead body. The woman was in shock. Seeing my police car, she raced across the street without looking, causing a garbage truck to lock up his brakes to avoid hitting her. I expected a woman in tears, but she was dry eyed. 'Officer, I think there's a dead person in the lot where my kids play. I'm not sure. It might be a mannequin, but I didn't want to get any closer.'

"I accompanied the woman back across the street and to the empty lot. The woman stopped a few steps into the lot, before the body was visible. She'd crossed her arms and gestured with her chin toward the farthest corner of the lot. 'Over there.' After determining that the gunshot victim was indeed dead, I called for detectives and the coroner's wagon before returning to the woman, who had her arms wrapped across her chest as if she was freezing, even though it was July and the air felt like a steam bath."

Jill nodded. "She was in shock."

"I took her elbow and steered her to the sidewalk where I took her name, address, and phone number. She'd appeared totally in control until I asked what the victim was wearing. The woman's vacant look followed, 'I don't know.'"

Jill nodded. "I remember Liz melting down when we found the spot where the Wupatki flood victims had been recovered. She'd never seen their bodies. But she melted down just seeing the spot where they were found."

We climbed into the pickup, and I made a U-turn. "As I recall, you were much less rattled at your first murder scene."

"Our murder scene was fresh. Jamie had just shot the guy doing the fake healing ceremonies on the Navajo reservation."

"You dealt with that well."

Jill turned toward me. "First of all, I am a ranch girl who's seen a lot of dead animals."

When she didn't go on, I asked, "What was the second part of that?"

"You didn't ask me to describe any of what I'd seen. I remember that the guy's face was partially missing, but I couldn't have described the vehicle, or anything about the scene. There's something about staring into his vacant eyes that made me think, 'His soul is gone. He's dead.'"

I followed the switchbacks in the road as we ascended from the lava flow, thinking about Jill's words. "His soul was gone? I thought that guy was a soulless bastard who'd killed at least one kid and had no remorse."

"Everyone has a soul, Doug. And when they die, it leaves their body."

"That sounds like a piece of Navajo wisdom Jamie Ballard might share."

"I think the concept of a soul is part of every religion. If you'd stayed awake through the sermons at church, you might remember that."

"It's my soul that's going to hell?"

"Don't kid about it, Doug. You may be a cynical cop, but heaven awaits."

"I'm not sure St. Peter will be as open-minded as you are."

Jill rode silently for a while. "What were the names of the guys who recovered the bodies?"

"Tonya said they were Rascal and…Gordo."

"What are you planning to ask them?"

"The people we've interviewed all offered the theory that the victims were hikers who bypassed a closed gate and walked the Chain of Craters Road to the lava flow. I'd like someone to tell me they had canteens, water packs, or other overnight gear."

Jill thought about my comments before answering. "The hiking theory is irrational. And it doesn't explain the victims' other injuries."

"Steve closed this investigation too quickly."

"Langevin suspected that the photographer had captured compromising images and didn't want anyone to see whatever is on the camera memory card."

Something tugged at the fringes of my brain. "There has to be more than a memory card. Photographers don't go anywhere without bringing a camera along. Let's find Rascal and Gordo. They might remember a camera or something that no one else remembers."

"Do you think they picked up a camera where the bodies were recovered?"

"Maybe." I guided Jill into a deserted part of the exhibits. "I've been thinking about Mocha. I have to get the US Attorney involved. We don't have access to any local resources, and dealing with money laundering and drugs outside of the park isn't our responsibility."

"I get it. I don't like it. But I get it."

"I'll call the US Attorney's Honolulu office."

"I'll meet you after I find a restroom."

Chapter 10

Sitting in the pickup outside of the visitors' center, I punched in the number for the US Attorney's Honolulu office while Jill went into the building in search of the women's restroom. After speaking to a receptionist, I was transferred to the administrative assistant of an Assistant US Attorney. After explaining who I was and providing the identification number from my Park Service credentials, I was put on hold.

"This is Andrew Linder. How can I help you, Mr. Fletcher?"

"I have a confidential informant who provided information about a drug smuggling and money laundering operation in Hilo. I need protection for her and contacts in the DEA and IRS."

"Mr. Fletcher, make an appointment with my admin and we'll discuss your situation and the informant."

"I'm Investigator Fletcher, from the National Park Service. This is an urgent and quickly evolving situation. I don't have time to make an appointment, fly from Hilo to Honolulu, and relay this information to you…at your convenience."

I envisioned a young lawyer, sitting in a small Honolulu office, trying to impress me with his power. In my mind, he was maybe twenty-five, just through with a judicial clerkship, and appointed because his daddy made contributions to the proper senate or congressional candidate.

"Listen, Investigator Fletcher, I don't discuss highly sensitive information over the phone, I don't know what in hell the NPS…whatever is, and I've never met or heard of you. If you want to talk, make an appointment and show up with your credentials. Otherwise, this conversation is over."

"Mr. Linder. I'm calling from an encrypted federal cell phone. A little blue light should be glowing on your phone. I provided my credentials to your admin, who certainly verified them before transferring the call to you. I work for the National Park Service Investigative Service Branch, the investigative arm of the Department of the Interior. If you're unable, or unwilling to speak with me, I'll have the director call his contact in the Attorney General's office and we'll work through them."

"Listen, Fletcher, I'm busy and I have no idea who you are. I'm going to call your bluff. Have your boss call whomever he thinks he needs to. I wish you luck with your drug and money laundering problems."

"Linder. How long have you had this job?"

"My tenure is irrelevant."

"I assume this is a stepping stone for you. If you like your current job possibilities, listen to what I've got to say. If you cut me off and this comes back to you through the IRS, DEA, or Attorney General, you're going to look like the quarterback who fumbled the ball on the one-yard line."

Linder paused so long I thought he'd hung up on me. "You've got fifteen seconds to tell me why I should care about what you heard from your informant."

"There are drugs and women being smuggled onto the Big Island. The money from the drugs and prostitution are being laundered through a Hilo strip club and a helicopter charter company."

Linder paused again. "Who's your director?"

"Jack Pardee. His office is in Salt Lake City. He reports directly to the Secretary of the Interior."

"Hang on for one minute."

I listened to classical music while watching tourists driving into the visitor center parking lot. Then, I wondered if Jill was feeling better or if she was lying on the floor of the women's restroom after throwing up or suffering through another bout of diarrhea.

"Fletcher, are you still there?"

"Yes."

"I have an order for you from the US Attorney. She says, 'Stand down.'"

"What? I have a confidential informant who's ready to supply details about drug smuggling and money laundering in return for transportation to the mainland."

"I conveyed your information to my boss, and she wants you to back away from whatever you're into."

Puzzle pieces swirled in my mind and suddenly came together. "This is part of something you're already pursuing."

"I take it that you're an experienced investigator, Fletcher."

"I was a detective for twenty years before joining the Park Service."

"Then you know that I can't answer your question."

"I'm going to pull my confidential informant out to protect her."

"No! Stand down. Step away from this line of investigation. That's an order."

"I'm sorry, Linder. You're breaking up. Give my boss a call and maybe he'll be able to get a better connection." I ended the call and turned my phone off.

I found Jill standing inside the door. "Are you okay?" I asked.

"Other than wondering if you'd fallen into the volcano crater, yeah, I'm fine. Did you speak with someone at the US Attorney's office?"

I took her elbow and guided her back to the pickup to have a private discussion. Once inside, I said, "They would prefer that we not get involved."

"What about Mocha?"

"We'll talk to her tomorrow."

"What are we going to tell her?"

"The US Attorney wants us to stand down."

"What? No. Mocha came to us scared, with a story that sounds plausible. We need to help her."

I held up my phone so the unlit screen was visible to Jill. "I think Jack will leave us a message about that."

"You can't turn your phone off. Jack will have a fit."

"What can he say? The battery died when it was exposed to the volcanic fog."

"Doug, you can be fired for insubordination and lose your pension."

"You suggested that we retire."

"Not now! Mocha confided in us."

"Then, we should have a plan when we talk to her tomorrow."

"What plan?"

"We've got about twenty hours to develop a plan."

"We were ordered to stand down."

"I'm not particularly good at following orders from people outside our chain of command."

"You were in the Army. Orders are orders."

"Technically, I was in the National Guard."

"You followed orders then. Did it matter if it came from your National Guard sergeant or someone in the regular army?"

"I was a private. I had no option but to follow orders regardless of the source. You told me that we're the civilian equivalent of lieutenant colonels. People at our level are expected to get orders, then use proper judgment in executing them. Officers who blindly follow orders get people killed."

Jill processed what I'd said, "We won't be killed, but Mocha's life is on the line."

"That's the nature of battle. The generals make decisions sitting far from the battle line, based on intelligence they're being fed. They issue an order, thinking it's the best overall plan, but it's up to the sergeant in the trenches to decide whether to rush into a hail of gunfire, or to make a flanking maneuver that accomplishes the objective without getting his squad killed."

"Don't you think Mocha's life is in danger?"

"If her boss finds out that she's cooperating with us, the best thing that could happen to her is for them to put a bullet into the back of her head."

Jill clenched her eyes shut. "Oh, God. If that's the best…" She looked up at me and nodded her understanding. "We need a plan."

"I agree," I said, opening the pickup door.

* * *

The ranger at the welcome desk directed us to a small door in the farthest corner of the visitor center, located behind a display panel. The muscular male ranger inside was inventorying the storeroom, which seemed to feature a mix of pamphlets, books, office supplies, and gear. He looked up from his clipboard when we opened the door.

"Visitors aren't allowed back here…" he paused when he saw the badge on my belt.

"Are you Rascal or Gordo?" I asked.

The man chuckled. "Rescue Rascal at your service. What brings two cops back here?"

Assessing the storeroom as one of the most secluded spots in the visitor center, I asked. "What can you tell us about the recovery you made from the lava flow?"

As I got closer to Rascal, I realized that his boyish looks, trim physique, and short beard made him appear younger than he was. A few gray hairs sprinkled his beard and temples. Setting aside his clipboard, Rascal pulled out three folding chairs. He opened the first one and set it in front of Jill. "Ma'am."

"I'm Jill Fletcher. This is my partner, Doug."

"The rangers call me Rascal," he said, shaking Jill's hand. "My name is Ralph Renfro." He sat in the third chair. "I've made a couple of rescues off the lava flow after the wind switched directions. We put on respirators then escort visitors who are coughing and wheezing. This is only the second time we've made a recovery of remains."

"What was unusual about these victims?" Jill asked.

"Well, they were unrecognizable. That made it gruesome, but actually less nightmarish. To be honest, I don't like handling dead people."

Nodding, I agreed. "That's not something we cops like either."

"It's part of the job," Rascal said, "but I..." He drew a breath. "I'm an adrenaline junkie. I get a rush from responding to a call out, but handling dead bodies isn't something I look forward to."

"Steve Langevin's report said the victims were hikers who'd bypassed the gate. What do you think?"

"That's odd. I'm sure they didn't walk down there. They didn't have any hiking boots. They were wearing athletic shoes."

Jill cocked her head. "What's your theory?"

Rascal leaned back in the chair, which seemed too small for his bulk. "To be honest, I felt their broken bones and smashed skulls. My first thought was that they'd been beaten and dumped by drug dealers after a deal went bad."

"Is that still your thought?" I asked.

"I don't know. The lava flow isn't accessible by boat, so someone would've had to unlock the gate, drive them down, drag their bodies a hundred yards across the lava, drive back, and relock the gate as they left. That seems unlikely."

"What's more likely?" I asked.

"This is wild, because the airspace was closed because of the laze cloud, but it almost appeared they'd been dropped from a plane or helicopter."

Jill straightened. "A helicopter?"

"I know it sounds crazy, but it would explain their broken legs and the bodies being miles from the nearest access point." When he didn't get an immediate response from us, he added, "I think some of the drugs get to the island by small planes and helicopters. Maybe there was a dispute during a drug delivery."

"The male victim was a photographer," I said. "Did you find a camera or other photographic gear?"

"We didn't find shit." Rascal paused and glanced at Jill. "Sorry."

"It's okay. I grew up on a ranch around cowboys. Shit was one of the milder swear words I've heard."

"The bodies were there, but nothing else. I mean, nothing." Rascal paused. "You know, the more I think about it, the helicopter thing seems more plausible. They were dropped out of a helicopter with nothing. That would explain a lot of things."

The storeroom door opened, and we all turned. "Hey Gordo, these guys are investigating the bodies we recovered from the lava flow."

Gordo was native Hawaiian, with a bodybuilder's physique. He nodded to us, apparently unsurprised to find two strangers in the storeroom. A man of few words, he said, "Weird shit."

I stood and offered my hand. "I'm Doug Fletcher and this is my partner, Jill. We're investigators from the National Park Service Investigative Services Branch."

"Like the FBI, only law enforcement rangers?" Gordo asked, pulling out another folding chair and sitting with us.

"Sort of," I replied. "We aren't law enforcement rangers. We're trying to fill in blanks on suspicious deaths and missing persons cases. Steve Langevin's report on the lava flow victims was a little thin."

Gordo rolled his eyes. "Steve."

"Don't you like Steve?" Jill asked.

Gordo shrugged. "He's a shit."

"That's kind of non-specific," I replied. "Is there something that soured you on him as a person or ranger?"

"Naw, he's just Steve."

I flashed back to my early Park Service days with Jamie Ballard, the Navajo National Police officer I grew to know and like over the course of two investigations. Jamie used words sparingly, even after we'd grown close. "Did Steve do something specific to irritate you?"

"Not really."

I looked at Rascal, who smiled. "Gordo is my silent partner."

Gordo nodded.

"I told them I thought the people had fallen out of a helicopter," Rascal said.

"A helicopter?"

"You know, the broken legs and smashed heads seem to fit with a fall from a helicopter."

"Interesting," Gordo replied.

"Do you think that's plausible?" Jill asked.

"Sure."

I tried to formulate an open-ended question that might tease a more expansive answer out of Gordo. "What's your theory?"

"The helicopter theory works for me."

"Why would they be in a helicopter? Then, how did they fall out?"

"Good question."

Jill's smile twitched. She was about to ask her own question when the radios carried by the two rangers both announced, "Fall at the caldera. Rescue call out."

Rascal and Gordo were out of their chairs before the second half of the message arrived. They were a well-oiled team; Rascal grabbed gloves and climbing ropes. Gordo pulled respirators, helmets, and climbing harnesses off a shelf behind me.

"Do you need our help?" Jill asked.

Rascal tossed two pairs of leather gloves to her. "If you can pull a rope, yes."

We followed through the visitor center lobby as rangers emerged from offices, hallways, and a break room. Visitors stood back as the group of rangers moved with urgency, but not panic. Gordo and Rascal threw their gear into the back of a pickup. Rascal climbed behind the wheel.

Gordo paused halfway in the passenger door and waved to us. "Get in the back."

Making sure not to hit any tourists who were now exiting the visitor center to watch the commotion, Rascal eased past the crowd until we were past the last car in the parking lot. It felt like we were riding in a jet during takeoff as I was pressed into the back seat by his acceleration.

"I thought the air was safe. Why are you bringing respirators?" Jill asked as she buckled in.

"Sulfur dioxide is heavier than air. The concentration is always highest at the bottom of the caldera."

Jill leaned forward and asked, "Will the person who fell be okay?"

Gordo looked over his shoulder. "Depends."

"Depends on what?" I asked.

"How far they fell. If they inhaled a lot of sulfur dioxide."

"Do you lose many visitors?" Jill asked.

Rascal looked at Jill in the mirror. "Not if we can help it."

Gordo looked over his shoulder at me. "A few."

"Isn't there a railing at the edge of the caldera?" I asked.

"Yep." Gordo replied.

"Then, how do they fall in?"

"Stupidity."

The two-mile drive took only two minutes despite the posted 10 mph speed limit.

A haggard Park Service volunteer was trying to keep the two-dozen visitors back from the railing.

Jill rushed forward to assist her crowd control efforts while the guys pulled gear out of the pickup bed. "What can I do?" I asked as Rascal and Gordo strapped on climbing harnesses, and helmets.

"Find out exactly where the kid went over."

I jogged to the group gathered at the railing. "Did anyone witness the fall?"

A young woman raised her hand. "We were taking selfies."

"Where?"

The woman pointed to a spot about twenty feet away. Scuff marks and a pink Nike cap were near the sharp edge of the caldera. "There," I pointed as Rascal arrived.

Gordo hopped over the waist-high railing like a gymnast and raced to the edge. Lying on his stomach he looked over the edge. "Fifty-foot ledge," he yelled to Rascal, who was tying the end of the climbing rope to the steel railing.

Rascal leaned close to me and whispered, "She's got a chance."

More Park Service vehicles raced into the parking lot, blocking in rental cars, as rangers ran to help move the crowd back. In the momentary distraction of their arrival, I didn't see Rascal rappel over the edge. Gordo put on a respirator, then followed a moment later.

A ranger bent under the railing, then crawled to the edge. Jill edged close to me. "Watching them peek over the edge creeps me out."

"Yeah, even knowing that the piece of lava she's lying on has been there for a thousand years doesn't reassure me."

The woman yelled something unintelligible to the climbers, her words lost in the wind. She slid back from the edge. "Zoey, get the Stokes stretcher and a second rope from Rascal's pickup."

A young ranger ran to the pickup and wrestled an aluminum basket from the back of the truck. A husky ranger helped her carry the 6-foot basket to the railing, then tied one end of the rope to the railing. Zoey checked his knot, then they donned leather gloves and together they slid the litter to the waiting rescue team.

Jill pressed leather gloves into my hand. "I doubt that they need help from old farts like us, but we can at least look like we're ready to help."

It took several minutes of rope work and yelling over the rim before Zoey signalled the assembled rangers. "We're ready for a lift."

The rangers lined up behind the railing as they pulled on leather gloves. Jill and I joined the line of rescuers who looked like they were prepared for a tug-of-war.

My shoulders and legs were cramping when the corner of the Stokes stretcher appeared at the edge of the caldera. Zoey and a male ranger reached over the crater rim and guided the litter over the edge as the rest of our team pulled it onto the flat surface next to the railing.

A ranger with a first aid pack stood by until the litter was safely clear of the rim. I saw more than heard the woman in the litter speaking to him after he removed the respirator Rascal and Gordo had fitted on her face. The young woman's verbal response gave me an emotional lift; we'd helped a rescue, not the recovery of a corpse. Two sirens, slightly out of sync with each other, whined in the distance.

I was ready to collapse when Zoey pointed to the other rope. "We're lifting Gordo first."

Jill looked at me. Having lost all her supper and not eaten breakfast at the B&B, she was done in. "Shit. It never occurred to me that the guys wouldn't just climb out." She sat down. "I'm done. Help them."

The rescue team came up more quickly than the stretcher, probably because they were climbing instead of the team pulling up the stretcher which was dead weight. Their uniforms were dripping with sweat, as they pulled off their respirators and helmets. The assembled team of rangers lined up to give them high-fives. Gordo walked up to me as he unsnapped his harness. "Did you help pull us up, old man?"

"I did."

Gordo nodded as an ambulance and Kona County police car arrived. "Thanks."

Steve Langevin, dressed in a police uniform, jogged to the assembled group around the Stokes stretcher. "Back up and let the EMTs through."

Gordo shook his head and snorted. "Good thing Steve arrived. He'll take care of everything."

"Do you have a history with Steve?" I asked.

"Steve has a history with everyone."

"What is that history?"

"He shows up after the work is done, then takes over."

Rascal removed his climbing harness and joined us, shaking his head. "It's a good thing Steve's here."

"He always takes charge?" I asked.

Rascal puckered like he'd sucked a lemon. "I don't mind him taking charge. The problem is his reports. They never give anyone credit, and they sound like he was the hero."

"But he isn't?" Jill asked.

"Steve conveniently arrives just after the work is done. It's like he's waiting in the wings until he's sure it's safe, then he rushes in to take over."

"I'm sure his boss knows," Jill replied.

Rascal looked around. "Gee, I don't see Superintendent Patton anywhere. He was probably in a Zoom meeting or working on the budget."

"He's conspicuously absent," Jill said.

"Patton's always too busy to be part of anything that might look bad," Gordo said.

Rascal chuckled. "He's a nephrocyte."

"I've never heard that word," I said.

"A nephrocyte is someone who's impeccably dressed, but totally incompetent."

Jill snickered. "I wonder if the rangers in Flagstaff called me a nephrocyte?"

I was about to say she had never been impeccably dressed when I tasted the flavor of my shoe. "You weren't incompetent."

Sensing my hesitation, Gordo, Jill, and Rascal all stared at me.

"I thought I saw Superintendent Patton."

"Yeah, right," Rascal said, smiling.

Pulling me aside, Jill and I walked away from the crowd. "You know that my third superpower is mind reading."

I drew a deep breath. The sulfur dioxide seemed more pungent than when we were nearer the rescue. "I didn't say anything inappropriate."

"You were about to say I wasn't impeccably dressed."

"Nope."

After rolling her eyes, Jill looked into the steaming caldera. "Do you think it's possible that the lava flow fatalities fell out of a helicopter, as Rascal suggested?"

Watching Steve move people out of the EMT's path, I shook my head. "I doubt it. Helicopters have doors and the passengers are belted in."

"Could they have fallen in this caldera, then their bodies moved by someone to the lava flow?"

"Getting this person out was a big production. I can't see how they could've fallen in here, been pulled up, then moved to the lava flow. Besides, the pathologist said they died from inhaling laze, which contains hydrochloric acid and silicon crystals. The caldera is full of sulfur dioxide. If I remember my high school chemistry, it turns into sulfuric acid when mixed with water."

"Then, we're back to the helicopter theory."

"I said…"

"A famous detective once said, 'When you've eliminated all that's impossible, then whatever remains, no matter how improbable, is the truth.'"

I closed my eyes and pinched the bridge of my nose. "That would be Sherlock Holmes, from *The Blanched Soldier.* It's fiction and Arthur Conan Doyle was high on cocaine when he wrote it."

"Our victims were a photographic crew. Doesn't it seem likely that they'd want the door open, so they could get clearer photos?"

"Fine. Even if they were flying in a helicopter with the door open, what idiot would unfasten his seatbelt? And why would the photographer's helper unfasten her seatbelt too? It's nuts! Besides, an ethical pilot would report the accident."

"He might not report it if he was somewhere he shouldn't have been. The park was closed because the Kona wind was blowing the laze cloud toward the island. His license might've been in jeopardy if he'd admitted to flying in closed airspace."

I tipped my head back, trying to come up with any other possible scenarios that would put the photographic crew high over the lava flow. "Why wasn't the helicopter pilot killed by the laze?"

"The area was clear while they were flying. The laze drifted in after the fall."

I stared at Jill. "Interesting."

"I wonder if helicopters have to file flight plans, and if they appear on the airport radar."

Jill was doing a search on her smartphone before I'd finished the question. "There are four helicopter tour companies on the Big Island. Paradise Helicopter Tours flies out of Hilo. I saw their heliport between Hilo and Volcano Village."

* * *

The Paradise Helicopter Tours receptionist looked up and smiled when we walked into the small office building adjacent to the hangar. "We're booked up today. I've got an opening tomorrow on one of our *doors off* flights."

Jill held out her Park Service credentials. "Actually, we have some questions."

The young woman, wearing a teal golf shirt with a helicopter logo embroidered on the left side looked uneasy. A sign on the desk indicated the woman's name was Dana. "I'm not really allowed to answer any questions. I just do the scheduling."

I smiled. "You've already answered one of our questions, Dana; you offer tours with the helicopter's doors open."

The woman eased slightly. "Um, yes. People who take pictures want tours with the doors open so they get sharper images. We offer one 'doors-open' tour each day."

"Do you file flight plans for your tours?" I asked.

"I don't think so. The pilot's have never mentioned flight plans. I think as long as they stay clear of the airport flight paths, we can fly anywhere over the island without a problem."

"Do the pilots communicate with the air traffic controllers?" I asked.

"I'm pretty sure they do. I mean, I've ridden on a few tours and the pilots always chatter with someone on the radio. Sometimes, it's up to other helicopters to find out where there's fog and what the winds are doing, but I think they talk to the airport too."

"Do you know if they are tracked on the airport radar?"

"I'm sure they are. The pilots talk about transponders. I think that's what the airports use to watch the helicopters."

"You didn't happen to lose a couple of tourists last week, did you?"

Dana cocked her head. "Lose?"

"Fell out of the helicopter."

"*What*? Are you kidding? If two people had fallen out of one of our helicopters, the NTSB and FAA would be on us like stink on shit. I mean, there'd be barricades across the driveway and inspectors going over every record, nut and bolt. The birds would be shut down, and the pilots would've been interviewed for days. Why would you even say something like that?"

"The two bodies recovered on the lava flow might've fallen from a helicopter."

"No way. That'd be all over the news."

Jill pulled a chair over from what appeared to be the area used to give pre-flight safety orientation to the customers. "Dana, how could something like that happen without the news finding out?"

"There's no way. None. The customers are strapped in, and they've all had safety orientation. Besides, no one sane would unbuckle themselves while we're flying. That's crazy. It's scary enough to just be up in the helo, especially during the open-door flights."

Jill leaned on her knees, looking very non-threatening. "Let's suppose that other tour operators are less…safety conscious, and they let a photographer unfasten his seatbelt."

Dana shook her head emphatically. She pointed to a framed certificate on the wall behind her desk. "The FAA is here quarterly to inspect our maintenance records and training procedures. We'd be out of business if we let someone unbuckle to take a better picture."

"Are there less ethical tour operators?" Jill asked.

"NO! We all have to comply with the same rules and regulations. Anyone who doesn't follow the rules would be out of business and the pilots would never fly a tourist again." Dana was wound up, so we let her cool off for a bit. The silence bothered her, and she stared off into the distance. "Where were the bodies found?"

"On the lava, near the spot where the lava is flowing into the ocean."

"And they were found last week?"

"Yeah. You probably read about it."

Dana turned her chair and typed into a computer keyboard. "Here's the story from the news. There's even a news helicopter video of the laze and lava flow." She switched screens and paged back through records. "First of all, we don't fly over the Park Service lava flow. We have to stay a quarter mile offshore. Secondly, there was a Kona wind that day, which blew the laze over the lava flow. No one would fly through that. It's deadly, and even if you lived, it'd cause all kinds of maintenance problems with the helicopter."

"Did you have any flights around the southern tip of the island that day?"

"Sure, every flight goes around the lava flow. It's a huge attraction and every tourist wants to take pictures of the steam rising when the lava hits the ocean."

"Did any of your pilots mention seeing a helicopter flying over the lava flow?'

"Not to me."

"Do they keep a flight log of information like that?" Jill asked.

"Their logs are flying hours, the number of passengers, fuel, maintenance concerns, and things like that."

"Who would they talk to about another pilot doing something dangerous or illegal?"

"I suppose they'd mention it to the owner or other pilots." Dana paused. "They'd probably notify the Kona airport tower, too."

"Could we talk to the pilots who flew that day?"

Dana spun around and pulled up the schedule. "Bruce is off today, and Greg is up with a tour. He should be back in twenty minutes. Judy just took off before you arrived, so she won't be back for two hours."

"Dana," Jill said softly. "The lava flow is a big tourist draw, so every helicopter tour flies near it, right?"

"Yes."

"When do the flights begin and end?"

"We start flying at ten in the morning and our last flight returns at six in the evening."

"Is that the same schedule the other companies fly?"

"There's a company out of Kahana, but the northwest resorts start flying at eight. They loop around Kona, so they don't get to the steam until about nine. I think everyone shuts down at the same time we do."

"I've seen pictures of the lava flowing after dark," Jill said.

"Those are professional photographers who charter flights. We don't take tourists out after dark."

I nodded. "The people whose bodies were found on the lava were professional photographers."

"They weren't flying with us," Dana replied. A second later, her eyes widened. "There's a guy who flies out of a ranch, way up in Waimea. He specializes in commercial work, like spraying and locating missing cattle who've wandered off. He also shuttles rich people between the islands. You know, people who don't want to arrive at the airport an hour before their flight, then go through security."

Jill leaned closer. "What rumors have you heard about him?"

"None of the tour operators will hire him because he doesn't have enough flight hours. We like retired military pilots who've logged thousands of hours at the controls. Gil went through a program at some California college and only has a few hundred hours of flight time."

"What's Gil's last name?" I asked.

"Jackson. Gil Jackson."

Jill glanced at me. We'd heard that name before.

Chapter 11

"How's your stomach?" I asked as we walked to the pickup.

"I'd eat a bowl of soup or a sandwich," Jill replied.

"There's a bag in the back with two muffins."

"They're probably dried out and hard."

I laughed as I started the engine. "If anything, this humidity has made them soggier."

Jill reached behind the seat and took out that bag. "It sounds like we should talk to Gil Jackson," she said as she peeled the waxed paper wrapper off a muffin. Jill stopped with the muffin halfway to her mouth. "Mocha said Gil Jackson was one of the people involved in the strip club money laundering."

I thought back to our discussion with Mocha. "You're right."

"I know I'm right. I feel like we just found a puzzle piece."

"Dana made an interesting comment about the helicopters being tracked on the Kona airport's radar. I'd like to see if the radar shows a helicopter veering over the lava rather than staying a quarter mile offshore."

"Mmm. This muffin melts in my mouth. I wish I had a cup of coffee to go with it."

"I saw a snack shop in Volcano Village. I'll get a sandwich and you can get a cup of coffee."

"Please don't get a tuna sandwich. I think that would make me lose it."

"Fried mahi mahi on a toasted bun sounds good."

"Really? I tell you that tuna might make me sick, so you decide that mahi mahi might be okay?"

"It's not tuna."

"Doug, it's fish. It'll stink and make me sick. Stick to a BLT or ham and cheese."

"I'll tell you what. I'll let you order for me, that way there won't be any issues, like the anchovies on Caesar salad."

Jill had a mouthful of muffin, so motioned for me to stop speaking. "You are so clueless," she said, wiping her mouth with a napkin from the bag. "Just mentioning Caesar salad is making me sick."

"Fine. I'll have a BLT. The mayo won't bother you?"

"There's no fish in mayo."

"No, but they put mayo in tuna salad sandwiches."

"Stop it!"

"Stop what?"

"I'm about one sniff of fish away from tossing my cookies and you keep mentioning…fishy things. Please, give it a rest."

* * *

I found a mom-and-pop Chinese restaurant in Hilo. Jill sniffed the aromas coming out of the door as diners exited and checked the menu before approving it. "There's shrimp on the menu. I think I can handle the smell of it in the restaurant if you don't order it."

"Right. No shrimp," I said, holding the door for her.

She ate chicken chow mein while I dove into an order of sesame chicken. "There aren't any vegetables in sesame chicken," she commented as she sprinkled soy sauce, then scooped up a forkful of rice.

"I love the tangy sweet sauce."

"It's just battered, deep-fried chicken with sauce."

"There are sesame seeds on top and rice on the side," I replied.

"I'm amazed that your body doesn't rebel against that fatty, no-fiber combination."

"My taste buds have overruled my gut's rebellion. It tastes good, so I eat it."

After an eye roll, Jill asked, "What's our next step?"

"I'm going to call the air traffic control supervisor at the Kona airport. I'd like to look at their radar records for the day the victims died."

"I think you're being overly optimistic about them giving you access to the radar history and what it might show."

"If your theory is correct, their radar history will show a helicopter flying over the lava flow after all the tours have ended."

"Will they let you see the radar?"

"I'm hoping he'll be overwhelmed by our credentials and your charm."

Jill snorted. "And if the supervisor is a woman and not overwhelmed by my charm?"

"We'll hope for the best."

Jill removed her smartphone from her pocket. I assumed she was searching for a phone number for the Kona air traffic control while I finished my meal. She punched in a number and handed me the phone. "I dialed the number for the Kona police office at the airport."

"Kona airport police. This is Officer Tanaka."

After introducing myself and explaining our interest in seeing the radar history from the estimated date and time of the hiker's deaths, Tanaka paused. "Here's the direct number for the control tower. Grace Akamu is the air traffic control supervisor."

Writing the number on a napkin, I thanked the officer and disconnected. "The supervisor is named Grace. Would you like to speak with her?"

"You can call while I finish the last bites of chow mein."

The person who answered the call put me on hold while he hailed the supervisor. I listened to classical music for two minutes before the call was reconnected. "This is Grace. How can I help you, Officer Fletcher?"

"Actually, I'm an investigator from the National Park Service looking into last week's suspicious deaths in Volcanoes National Park. We're exploring the possibility that the victims may have fallen from a tour helicopter. I'd like to look at the air traffic radar for the evening of their deaths."

"The news said the victims were hikers."

"The coroner's report indicated that they'd fallen quite a distance before they died on the lava. Their legs were shattered."

"Oh, dear. That's…bizarre. You think they might've been pushed from a helicopter?"

"That's one of the possibilities we're investigating."

"I'd be happy to show you that radar record when you bring the search warrant."

"The whole helicopter scenario is a little far out. I was hoping you'd let us look at the radar without having to find a judge to sign a search warrant. Did I mention that we're federal investigators?"

"Did I mention that the radar images are sensitive data protected from casual use by a federal law?"

"But there are websites that allow people to watch the locations of planes in the air."

"Have you ever watched your plane's route during a flight?"

"Sure."

"Would you rely on the accuracy of that image to guide you to the airport while making sure there are no other planes at your altitude within a few miles?"

I sighed. "Is your radar more accurate?"

"It has to be to ensure the safety of the airspace."

Jill was writing a note on a paper napkin as I spoke. She pushed the napkin to me. "Ms. Akamu, can you look at the radar from that time period and tell me if there's a helicopter over the lava?"

"I'm in a busy control tower, Inspector Fletcher."

"Your peek at the radar could save me a day of drafting a search warrant and a trip to Honolulu to have a federal magistrate sign it." When she didn't reply immediately, I added, "And you looking at the radar and telling me if there was something significant wouldn't involve me seeing sensitive information."

She sighed. "Hang on."

"Well," Jill asked.

"She's thinking about it."

I listened to classical music while Jill cleared our table and got refills of green tea. It was nearly fifteen minutes later when Grace Akamu's voice interrupted the music.

"What's the NPSISB?" Akamu asked.

"What?"

"Your caller ID says 'NPSISB?' What does that stand for?"

"We're part of the National Park Service Investigative Services Branch. Think of us as the Park Service version of the FBI."

"As unlikely as it seems, there *was* a helicopter transponder transmitting from the area over the park for nearly fifteen minutes."

"What time did that occur?"

"It was during sunset. They hovered in the area, then sped north across the park. By the way, that's against the rules. The helicopters are supposed to stay offshore."

"Did you report them to the park or the FAA?"

"I wasn't in the control tower when that happened. They didn't pose a risk to any other airborne traffic, so I assume the air traffic controllers who were on duty made a quick risk assessment and moved to more pressing matters."

I nodded to Jill. "Can you tell me which company owned that helicopter?"

"All I have is the helicopter's transponder ID. You'll have to get the ownership information from the FAA."

"Great! I can do that," I said, writing down the information.

"And Fletcher, if you need this radar information for a court case, you'll have to get a search warrant."

"Of course," I replied. "Thank you."

"One other thing. That helicopter doesn't belong to one of the tour companies. My controller said he sees that transponder making multiple trips between the islands several times a week. It must belong to someone who's running an inter-island charter business."

"That helps a lot. Thank you."

Akamu chuckled. "Let me know if this solves a murder…and include my name in your report. It'd be nice to get some positive recognition."

I ended the call and handed the phone back to Jill. "Look up helicopter charters on the Big Island."

"All the tour companies offer charters."

"Is there one that doesn't cater to the tourist business? Maybe one advertising executive inter-island transportation?"

"The Waimea Transport website says they specialize in custom inter-island charters and commercial work. Guess who it lists as the contact?"

"Gil Jackson. How far are we from Waimea?"

Jill punched information into her smartphone. "Waimea is a two hour and twelve-minute drive if we go up the east coast and loop around the north end." Jill paused. "I don't think we should approach Jackson before we decide what to do about Mocha."

Looking at my watch, I realized it was already mid-afternoon. "You're right. We might be putting Mocha's life in danger if we question him. Let's go back to the B&B, brainstorm about Mocha's situation and look at the rest of the video and pictures on the chip."

* * *

The aroma of fresh-baked cookies greeted us when I opened the front door of the B&B. Set out on a sideboard, under a wall-mounted television, were cups on a serving tray, a thermal coffee carafe, and a platter of white-chocolate chip cookies sat on tiny napkins. I was pumping coffee into a cup when our hostess appeared.

"You found the cookies."

Jill waved her cookie while chewing. "These are wonderful. Can I get the recipe?"

"Sure, but macadamia nuts are sometimes hard to find on the mainland."

Jill was about to bite into her second cookie when Mary smiled. "Be careful, Jill. The locals have a saying, 'One macadamia nut is good. Two is better. Three is diarrhea.'"

Stopping mid-chew Jill's eyes went wide. "You're kidding, right?"

"Macadamia nuts are high in fat and fiber. Many people use them as a natural laxative and some of the spas use a macadamia nut smoothie to stimulate a colon cleanse."

I took the second cookie from Jill's hand. "After this morning's episode, I think your colon is clean enough."

"Killjoy," she whispered as she wiped her fingers on a napkin.

"Have you solved the mystery of the dead hikers?" Mary asked.

"The investigation is ongoing," I replied.

"Keep in mind, Hilo is a small town. News travels fast. If you've been asking questions, the locals will hear about it quickly."

"Can you be discreet?" Jill asked.

Laughing, Mary picked up a cookie and took a bite. "I won't repeat anything you ask me to hold in confidence until after I hear it on the news."

"What do you know about Gil Jackson?"

Mary's smile disappeared and she set the remainder of her cookie on a napkin. "He lives up north, near Waimea."

"We saw that he runs a helicopter charter."

"That's true."

"What else can you tell us about him?" Jill asked.

Mary sat and patted the couch, gesturing for Jill to sit alongside her. "Gil spends more than his helicopter business makes."

"Lots of people are overextended," I replied, leaning against the buffet table. "I think most of the people in the United States are one paycheck away from bankruptcy."

Mary's lack of reaction was telling. "Doug, Mr. Jackson drives a BMW and owns two helicopters. The bank president is a schoolmate of mine. Gil doesn't have loans on his helicopters, car, or house. They're all paid off. Nobody makes that kind of money by helping ranchers find lost cattle and occasionally flying a businessman to Honolulu."

"We heard that he shuttles businessmen between all the islands."

"Who told you that?"

"Our sources are…"

Mary stopped me. "I've heard that Gil flies between the islands, but there's rarely a male passenger in his helicopter."

Jill leaned back. "A suspicious person would speculate that he's in the drug and human trafficking business."

"Since I don't use drugs or hire prostitutes, I won't comment."

"But you've overheard people speculate about Mr. Jackson's activities."

"People often speculate about things they know nothing about."

"Maybe Mr. Jackson inherited some money from a rich relative," I said.

Mary clasped her hands in her lap and stared at me. "Gil Jackson parties in circles that are known to include the rich and famous. I've seen him pictured with celebrities who've been through rehab so many times they've earned frequent flier credits toward future stays."

"Are you saying he's into drugs?" Jill asked.

"I think he's smarter than that. And I don't think hard drugs mix well with piloting a helicopter. If I had to guess, I'd say he supplies the drugs."

"You mentioned female helicopter passengers," Jill said.

Mary cocked her head. "I've heard his passengers tend to be pretty young women dressed in skimpy outfits. They're usually whisked away in expensive cars after departing the helicopter."

Thinking about the video we'd started watching, I asked, "Do you have a picture of Gil?"

"I assume his helicopter business has a website with his picture." Mary paused. "Why do you want to see his picture?"

"It might be helpful if we bump into him somewhere."

Mary stood and smiled. "You won't bump into Gil. He prefers private parties to hanging out in bars and restaurants with the locals."

A wave of revelation swept over Jill as Mary walked away. "Gil has too much money, he flies young women between the islands, and he attends private parties with the rich and famous."

Mary stopped at the kitchen doorway. "I think Jill has connected the dots."

I nodded toward our room before Jill said anything more. I closed and locked the door. "It appears that Mr. Jackson is distributing drugs, is human trafficking, AND he's Mocha's boss at the strip club where he's laundering the money."

"Like Mary said, this is a small island. He's got to be on some police agency's radar." A look of understanding swept Jill's face. "That's why you were ordered to stand down when you mentioned your informant and money laundering."

I pointed to Jill's laptop. "Look up Gil Jackson's business website so we can see his picture."

Jill looked at me as the computer went through its warmup. "What are you thinking?"

"We were watching a video of a private party where drugs were being used and sold. I wonder if Mr. Jackson will show up in the video with Steve Langevin."

Twenty minutes later, we were well into the video of the party when Jill froze the screen. "That's Gil Jackson with the blonde in the skimpy bikini."

"Restart the video."

We watched as twenty or more people drank, laughed, swam, and wandered in and out of the house behind the camera. Jill gasped and looked away from the screen. "That couple on the right…"

"They're pretty uninhibited," I said, intrigued by their near-naked bodies and bumbling attempt to shield their drug use from the other partygoers.

"That's way past uninhibited. They're…"

"They're rich exhibitionists, under the influence of whatever they're snorting, and maybe…"

Jill stopped the video and pointed at the screen. "That's Gil watching them."

"And that's Steve Langevin talking to a spaced-out guy in the background."

"Gil's not under the influence of anything but voyeuristic lust."

"That's…disgusting." Jill shut down the video. "I don't need or want to see any more."

"Look at the files again. Check the dates. Unless I'm mistaken, the most recent pictures on this card are like two-weeks old."

"So?" Jill asked.

"Our photographers were taking pictures the night they died. This is not the card that was in the camera the day they fell. We're missing a camera and the most recent pictures associated with it."

"It wasn't listed with the victim's personal effects," Jill said as she checked the file dates.

"And it wasn't mentioned by the rangers who discovered the bodies or the recovery team."

"Do you think it's still in the helicopter?"

"Not if it was in the photographer's hands when he was pushed or fell. I think it might still be laying out on the lava."

"No one saw it," Jill replied.

"Think about how uneven and cracked the surface of the lava is. The lava left grooves and crevices everywhere as it oozed toward the ocean. We need to go back and search the area where the bodies were found." I stood, expecting Jill to get up.

"It's been a long day. Let's hit it hard in the morning."

Looking at Jill's pale face I said, "I suppose you're out of gas. You haven't eaten much today."

"And I suppose you're hungry. It's nearly six o'clock."

"The sugar rush from the cookie is gone. My stomach is grumbling. We could go back to the bar and check out tonight's special."

"The mom-and-pop sushi place has miso soup and pho on the menu. That might be a better option for me than the catch of the day."

I held the door as Jill stood. "There might be fish smells there. Are you up for that?"

"Smells are okay now. I just want something gentle on my stomach and soup sounds like a good option."

Jill had her phone out as soon as I backed out of our parking spot. "Hi Jack, do you have a minute for a Hawaii update?"

Jill activated the phone's speaker function and held it between us. "I'm here with Doug on the speaker."

"I've left Doug several messages. I suppose his phone's battery died."

"I was having some problems with it during an earlier call. The cell coverage here is spotty and it didn't get a full charge last night."

"I understand you had a discussion with an Assistant US Attorney who told you to step away from something you were pursuing. I hope you're heeding that advice."

"Yeah, we have plenty on our plates with the deaths of the people on the lava."

I nodded to Jill, who took over the update. "We've made some progress. The victims fell from more than a few feet, and one of the rescue team members suggested that the victims may have fallen from a helicopter. We've identified the helicopter pilot who was probably flying over the lava flow at the time of our victims' deaths."

"Have you questioned him?"

I leaned toward the phone. "I think that might lead us too close to whatever the US Attorney is investigating. A local contact gave us information that the helicopter pilot may be an inter-island smuggler and money launderer. The camera memory card found with the remains has a video taken by our victims of a party he attended in the weeks before their deaths."

Jill added, "It appears that the helicopter pilot and one of our seasonal rangers may have been providing drugs for the party."

"A ranger too?"

I leaned toward the phone. "It appears that the ranger exchanged drugs for a handful of cash, but it was done discreetly. No prosecutor would take him to court based on the video we saw, but I'm 99% sure we watched a drug deal."

"Shit," Jack said. "How are you going to deal with that?"

"The memory card found with the victims' remains doesn't have the most recent photos taken by the photographers. Tomorrow, we're going back to the area where the bodies were found. The terrain is irregular and off the beaten path, so the camera may have fallen into a crack or depression in the lava. I hope the most recent pictures may be more revealing."

"Are you providing this information to the local police?"

I hesitated. "That may be a problem. The seasonal law enforcement ranger is also a part-time local cop."

There was a pause before Jack replied. "If you're uneasy about dealing with the local police, bring in the FBI or DEA. I don't want you two going after the bad guys alone."

Jill gave a nervous chuckle. "Don't worry. I don't need to be anywhere around when the arrests are made. I'm having nightmares from our last two cases."

"I'm relieved to hear that. I was beginning to think you two were trigger happy. You've discharged your firearms more in the past year than all the rangers in the entire remaining National Park Service, and that includes the rangers in Yellowstone and Glacier National Parks who've had to put down a few injured or dangerous animals."

"Got it. No gun play in Hawaii," Jill said.

I slid the phone over to me. "Jack, we have a confidential informant with information about drug smuggling and money laundering. As you know, the Assistant US Attorney talked to his boss, who ordered us to stand down. We fear for the life of our informant, and we'd like to develop a plan to extract her."

"I assume the attorneys were just as circumspect with you as they were with me. They want us out of the way, but they won't say why or how quickly they plan to act on whatever information they have."

"That's more than I got. All I got was an order to stand down and a threat to call my boss."

Jack sighed. "We can't upset a big multi-agency operation. On the other hand, if you feel your informant's life is in danger, I can see why you'd like to act."

"And?"

"And what?" Jack asked.

"Can we pursue our investigation and the removal of our informant, or do we have to stand down?"

"Jeez, Doug, how can you even ask that question? A US Attorney ordered you to stand down. That doesn't leave any wiggle room."

"She's not in my chain of command. Are you ordering me to not pursue the case with full vigor?"

"Matt warned me that you liked to push the envelope." Jack sighed. "I can't overrule the US Attorney. I have to assume they've got a broader operation and you're stepping into the fringes of what they're doing. On the other hand, they're not forthcoming about the operation and they haven't invited our participation. Go ahead with your investigation of the murders but try not to stray into whatever they're doing."

"How can I do that when they won't tell us what they're doing?"

"Use your best judgment."

Jill disconnected the call and looked at me. "You didn't say much after Jack told you to use your best judgment. Nor did you say anything after he suggested that we not get involved in another armed confrontation."

"My experience with drug dealers and smugglers is that they own lots of guns, and they don't hesitate to use them."

"Like Jack suggested, we'll leave the investigation with the FBI or DEA and let them make the arrest." When I didn't immediately respond, Jill smiled. "It really sticks in your craw when you do all the work and hand the case over to the FBI who makes the arrest."

I sighed. "Yes, but Jack's right. The Park Service is not primarily a police agency. The FBI, DEA, and US Marshals all have armed arrest teams who deal with drug dealers all the time. They have body armor and experienced teams. We're not accustomed to confronting heavily armed drug dealers and murderers."

Jill smirked. "Who kidnapped my husband and put this stranger in the truck with me?"

"Ha ha. As much as I like to be part of closing the case involving Mocha, our last two cases have been more exciting than I'd prefer."

"What are we going to say to Mocha? We can't tell her that other agencies told us to stand down."

"Maybe we'll put her on a Hilo fishing boat and send her on a two-week charter."

"That sounds like a lovely plan, dear. Maybe they'll rescue Gilligan and the Skipper while they're out."

"I always liked Mary Ann the best."

"Focus, Doug. We need to talk to Mocha tomorrow and telling her to wait for other agencies isn't going to be an acceptable response."

"My mom always told me to sleep on problems and the answer would be clear in the morning."

"Great. You get to 'sleep on it' while I spend the whole night tossing and worrying about Mocha."

"I've got nothing right now."

"So, we'll brainstorm. Throw out some ideas."

"I suggested rescuing Gilligan. It's your turn."

"Let's take her to the airport and put her on a plane."

"Whose expense account is that going on?"

"I paid for the hay at Tuzigoot. It's your turn."

"You were prepared to pay for the hay out of your own pocket if the expense voucher was refused. I'm not paying for a one-way ticket to…wherever. What's your next idea?"

Jill tipped her head back and thought. "We can put her up in a hotel on the other side of the island."

"You heard Mary. This whole island is a small town. Everyone knows each other and all the secrets."

That comment got me a glare. "You know that the point of brainstorming is to build off other people's ideas, not to shoot them down. Right?"

"When you have something I can build on, I'll build. I won't…"

"You won't, what?" Jill stared at me for a second, then rolled her eyes. "You tasted shoe leather before you even got the words out, didn't you?"

"I'm more situationally aware than I used to be." I turned the truck into a parking lot. "Oh look. We're at the soup restaurant. I wonder if they have anything that will stick to my ribs. The sesame chicken was gone about an hour after I ate it."

I looked at Jill who was biting her lip.

"What?"

"You don't appreciate my dietary advice."

"I'll see if they will prepare something with one stalk of broccoli in it."

"That'll be one more vegetable than you had for lunch. It'll satisfy your hunger longer than the breaded sesame chicken, plus provide some fiber and vitamins."

"I'll ask for lemon to put into my tea. That way I won't get scurvy."

Jill rolled her eyes so far back I thought she was checking her scalp for dandruff. "I suppose that's a start."

We talked about the house, Matt and Mandy, and our parents over my stir-fried beef and broccoli and Jill's egg drop soup. Mocha's situation was the elephant in the room that we ignored for the evening.

Back at the B&B we prepared for bed and watched the local news, which included discussion of the woman who was rescued from the volcano caldera. The Hawaiian weather forecast was a repeat of the previous day aside from a discussion of the trade winds returning.

"I could be a forecaster here," I said as I shut off the television. "Every day it gets into the 80's and there's a chance of an afternoon shower."

Jill didn't comment, instead rolling onto her side facing away from me.

I snuggled into her back. "Are we okay?"

"Of course, *we're* okay. I'm just worried about Mocha."

"I was afraid I'd put my foot into my mouth one too many times."

Rolling over so we were nose to nose, Jill stared into my eyes. "You're still the Doug I married and love, even if you're a little short on diplomacy, sometimes."

"Only sometimes?" When Jill didn't immediately respond I added, "You get a little frustrated with me, sometimes."

"I do. And sometimes I express my frustration a little too emphatically. I think that comes from living alone for so many years. When I was single, I let my frustrations out by yelling at the walls. Now, I focus my rants on you. I hope you understand that it's not personal."

"I developed a thick skin. But you need to let me know if I'm not reacting to something that's important to you."

"Mocha is important to me. We need to find a resolution to her problem."

"We've been told to stand down by the US Attorney and our boss. I think that message is loud and clear."

Sighing, Jill kissed me. "I know. I just wish there was something…"

"Maybe something will miraculously change tomorrow."

"I guess that's all we can tell Mocha. 'Hang in there. We're hoping for a miracle.'"

"Hey, miracles happen. Look at us; despite the odds, we found each other." I pulled her close.

"Easy, cowboy. My stomach isn't entirely settled."

"Okay then. I guess romance is off the table for tonight."

Jill touched the side of my face and smiled. "You told me to be honest with you about important things. Nausea is a romance killer."

I chuckled. "That's a compelling argument." I kissed her gently. "You had a tough day. I hope you feel better in the morning."

Chapter 12

After a delicious omelet that Jill sampled, then passed to me, and warm banana bread, we took our coffee cups to the patio. Mary brought a coffee carafe and nodded toward the bougainvillea, "Should I bring another cup?"

Jill nodded. "That would be nice. Thank you."

Mary paused at the door. "The girls are mostly quiet neighbors, but I don't approve."

I topped off my coffee. "Most of them didn't make a choice to be in the business. Once they're in, it's hard to get out."

Mary shivered like she'd felt a sudden chill. "I pray for them."

"Some prayers are answered," Jill replied.

Mary left a third cup without responding. I leaned toward the pink flowers of the bougainvillea. "I've got a cup of coffee for you."

I heard faint rustling and a chair squeaked on the other side of the bush. A moment later Mocha appeared, this time wearing a see-through coverup over a chartreuse bikini. She glided to the chair next to Jill and sat down as I poured her a cup of coffee.

"What's the plan?" Mocha asked as Jill passed the coffee to her.

"How soon do you need to leave?" Jill asked.

"About five years ago would've been good," Mocha replied as she cupped the coffee mug in her hand and leaned back in the chair.

"When you were seventeen?" Jill asked.

Mocha laughed. "You're good, girl."

Jill didn't crack a smile but asked, "Can we get you into a rehab facility as part of the deal?"

Mocha crossed her ankles, reflexively trying to hide the needle tracks under her beach shoes. "Rehab?"

"What's your drug of choice?" I asked. "You have all your teeth, so it's not meth. Cocaine is sourced out of South America and Mexico, so it's probably hard to get here. I suppose a shipment of opium or heroin coming out of the Far East is probably easier to procure than any other opiate."

Ignoring my question, Mocha sipped her coffee. "I need to leave before this weekend."

"Why this weekend?" Jill asked.

"Like I told you, there's a party for a bunch of Asian businessmen. They like blondes, but they're curious about dark-skinned girls, like me."

"Curious?" Jill asked.

Mocha closed her eyes. "Use your imagination, then add elements of disgust, horror, and pain."

Jill set her coffee cup on the table, closed her eyes, and crossed her arms. "I've led a sheltered life."

Mocha chuckled. "Your White life in the little house on the prairie wouldn't prepare you for the things I've seen…and done."

"Or had done to you," I added.

Mocha's expression hardened. "I forgot that you were a cop. You've seen it, haven't you, Doug?"

"I'm afraid so. Bodies in cheap hotel rooms, hospitals, and alleys."

Jill sat up and reached for the carafe. "Let's get back to plans," she said, pouring coffee into all our cups.

"How are you getting me out?" Mocha asked. "Are you taking me from here, or are the marshals coming for me? Are all the girls included in the deal, or just me?"

"I spoke with the Assistant US Attorney. The plans haven't been formalized, but we're working on it. Are you willing to testify against Jackson and Langevin?"

Mocha pushed up her sunglasses and stared at me. "I want to leave and never come back."

"That's not how witness protection works. You're put into a local safe house until the trial is over. Then, you get a new identity and are relocated to some out of the way place."

"I can tell you where the books are and how they're laundering the money. That should be enough to put them away."

"They'll want you on the witness stand to explain how the money was moved around and who was involved."

"I don't think I can do that. I mean…they'll kill me before I'll ever get to the witness stand. These are terrible people, Doug. I can tell you where bodies are buried…literally." Mocha started to fidget, then stood. "I've got to go. If you can't help me…"

Jill stood and put her hand on Mocha's arm. "We won't let anything happen to you. Keep yourself together for a couple more days. Okay?"

"If you can't get me out of here by Saturday morning, I'll leave on my own."

"I thought you didn't have any money?" I asked.

Mocha glared at me. "I've got assets to trade for transportation. It won't be pleasant, but it might be better than another Asian pool party."

Mocha disappeared around the bougainvillea bush, leaving Jill staring at the spot she'd disappeared. "What did she mean about having assets to trade for transportation?"

"I suspect she's willing to trade sexual favors for transportation on a ship."

Jill's mouth fell open, unable to express her disgust.

"I think Mocha is that desperate."

"We've got to get her out of here."

"We don't have a plan and we've been ordered to stand down."

Jill tipped her head back and looked at the wispy clouds. "Call Jack."

"Jack's got his whole career ahead of him. He's going to tell us the same thing he said last night."

Jill sat down facing me. "Okay, Fletcher. What's plan B?"

"We hope that someone in the US attorney's office brings us into whatever case they've got going."

"That's plan A and it's not working. What's plan C?"

"We use our personal credit cards to buy a one-way ticket to San Francisco on Friday night."

"That sounds like a terminal plan. As in, we'll be terminated."

"How badly do you want to get Mocha out of here?"

"This sucks. It shouldn't be this hard to do the right thing."

"The right thing and the legal thing are sometimes in conflict."

* * *

Jill decided to talk about something other than Mocha on the way to the park. "The Spam and cheese omelet Mary served us was…interesting. I haven't had Spam since I was a kid."

"I've heard that Hawaii consumes more Spam than any other state, including Minnesota, where it's made."

"That seems odd."

"I guess it became a local staple during WWII when meat was scarce. Lots of Spam was shipped to the troops. Some of it was distributed to the protein deprived Hawaiian civilians, who developed a taste for it."

"It's kind of salty for my taste," Jill replied.

"It's comfort food here, like your mother's biscuits and gravy."

"What's your plan for when we get to the visitor center?"

"I hope we can find Zoey, the ranger who found the victims. I'd like her to take us to the exact site where the bodies were found."

The ranger at the welcome desk directed us to the display area where Zoey was answering visitors' questions. She nodded to us when we approached, then walked over when she'd finished with the questions.

"Good morning. Have you solved the mystery yet?"

Jill smiled and held her finger and thumb about an inch apart. "We're this close. Can you drive us down to the lava flow and show us exactly where you found the bodies?"

Zoey looked around. "It's quiet here, so I should be able to break free for an hour or so. I'll get the keys to one of the pickups and meet you in the parking lot."

A few visitors passed and Jill waited until they were out of earshot. "I don't know that I'd be happy to show a couple of cops the site where I'd found dead bodies."

"Zoey seemed okay with it. Let's hope she doesn't get squeamish when we approach the site of the discovery."

My cell phone buzzed, the caller ID showing NPSISB. "It's Jack," I said as I accepted the call.

"Wow, you've actually got your phone charged and turned on."

"I got the directive from headquarters."

"I got a call from the US Attorney in Honolulu. She had the impression that you were about to mess up something they've been pursuing. I understand her assistant, who ordered you to stand down, got the impression that you might not comply."

"It's complicated."

Jack coughed. "Jeez, Doug. Are you seriously considering disobeying a stand down order from the Department of Justice?"

"We don't report to them."

"No, but they prosecute the cases we bring them. I've always felt it was best to stay on their good side." Jack paused, then added, "Is this another of your out of bounds plays to get around the government bureaucracy?"

"A woman approached me with information about a human trafficking, money laundering, and drug smuggling operation. She asked Jill and me to get her off the island in return for information about the other operations. She's within days of being put in an untenable position and may flee if we don't act."

"Did you explain that to the attorney?"

"Jack, the recent law school grad shithead I spoke with has no street experience and no respect for the gravity of the situation. He's never seen what happens to a prostitute who flees her pimp. He asked me to make an appointment with his admin assistant so I could fly to his Honolulu office and discuss the matter."

"And you feel this woman's life is in danger?"

"Mocha told us this morning that she has to leave before Saturday. If we can't help her, she's going to jump onto a ship and leave. It sounds like that'll effectively remove the DOJ's best witness and the person who knows how the money flows and where the bodies are buried."

"She'll need a passport if the ship is going somewhere other than the US mainland."

"Jack, she's afraid she's going to be killed. A passport is irrelevant when you think you're about to die."

"Matt said you have a way of stepping on toes and not waiting for the bureaucrats to catch up."

"I didn't get a sense of urgency from the US attorney's office. Talk to them, Jack. If the DEA or FBI has an operation going on, great. Have them read us in, we'll explain the need for urgency, and we'll play along…if they can help my confidential informant before she's killed or jumps on a boat or plane."

"I'll make the call, but I got the impression that the DOJ isn't interested in having the Park Service as part of their team."

"Jack, it's not *their* team. We all work for the same government. We all swore the same oath to uphold the Constitution and enforce the law. Jill and I are federal law enforcement officers. We have badges, guns, and security clearances. We aren't park rangers teaching children about ecology, nor are we ticketing litterers."

"Yeah. Yeah. I'll make the call."

"Jack, be the driver. Don't ask permission, tell them that we're part of the team. Advise them that we will act on this before Saturday, with or without them."

"They may not take that well."

"Then they'd better be prepared to handcuff two of your people and put us in the federal lockup." I ended the call before Jack could respond.

Jill didn't look pleased. "You came on a little strong."

"You're the one who encouraged me to implement plan C or D."

* * *

Zoey showed up smiling with a set of keys dangling from her fingers. "Are we ready to go?"

She drove us through the old lava fields past signs showing dates the exposed dark lava had flowed through different areas along the road. The lava flows became more recent as we descended toward the ocean. Turning to the left, we drove out of the foliage exposing the billowing cloud of steam blowing out over the ocean.

"Wow, this is even more spectacular than the other day," Jill said. "This is incredible. I've never seen anything like this except at Yellowstone National Park."

"We're still a mile away," Zoey replied. "Just wait until we're standing on the lava."

We traveled a switchback road that cut down a steep hillside, then drove across the lava field to a road running parallel to the coastline. The dark black layer indicated that we were driving over relatively fresh lava.

"How old is this lava, Zoey?"

"In geological terms, this is fresh lava, but realistically, this flow is older than I am."

Jill glanced at Zoey, then mouthed, "She's not thirty."

Feeling the hairs on my neck start to rise, I asked. "Are we in danger of being caught in a lava flow here?"

"There's no risk of the lava flowing here. It's running through lava tubes east of here, then flowing into the ocean. Our bigger risk is from this shelf breaking off."

"What shelf?" I asked, looking around at the continuous black rock field running a hundred yards beyond the road, toward the ocean.

"This area is where lava flowed over the ocean. Because it solidified when it reached the water, the new lava pushed outward creating a shelf over the ocean water."

"We're driving on a shelf? Are we in danger?"

"Probably not. Just to be safe, we'll park on the *makai* side of the road."

"We're parking on the side toward the hill in hopes that we'll be safe if the lava shelf breaks away in the middle of the road?"

Zoey glanced at me in the rear-view mirror. "It's physics."

"Pretend I didn't take calculus," I said. "Explain the physics."

"We're on a cantilevered ledge that's attached to the island near the base of the hillside. The pickup exerts more force the farther we get from the hill. By parking on the *makai* side of the road, we're exerting less downward force on the ledge."

"You think parking thirty feet closer to the hillside will make a difference?"

"Sure, the truck weighs like two thousand kilograms and placing it ten meters farther from the fulcrum of the cantilevered ledge exerts an additional…"

Jill put her hand on Zoey's arm. "Don't bother explaining. Doug was being sarcastic."

Obviously sad that she couldn't show off her physics knowledge and ability to do the force calculation in her head, Zoey said, "Oh."

After parking near a small hut and consulting with the ranger inside, Zoey led us to a spot where the blacktop ended abruptly under a waist high lava flow. A twisted signpost embedded in lava thirty meters from the end of the pavement displayed the message, NO PARKING.

Yelling to be heard over the roar of the lava boiling the ocean water into steam a few hundred yards away, Zoey said, "Follow the yellow tabs." She climbed some rocks that had broken free from the lava flow. "We check the temperature of the surface daily to make sure the marked pathway doesn't have a lava tube flowing under it."

Jill nimbly mounted the rocks, then looked back at me. "C'mon."

"I'm not reassured that there was no lava flowing under the trail this morning. Things change."

Zoey paused, waiting for me to climb onto the lava flow. "Is there a problem?"

Jill turned and smiled, yelling, "Doug's hemorrhoids are acting up."

A couple returning from their walk to the edge of the lava flow overheard the exchange, then looked at me. I nodded, like I was reassured. As they passed, I said, "That's Park Service code for safe lava."

We followed Zoey about one hundred yards. She stopped and looked around before pointing to a spot parallel to the edge of the lava but away from the ocean. "We found the man's body over there."

"There aren't any yellow markers over there," I pointed out as Zoey was about to depart from the marked trail.

"It's safe," she yelled. "The recovery team walked back and forth across this lava sheet several times when they recovered the bodies."

"Is it safe beyond this area?" I asked.

Sensing my apprehension, and seeing Jill's smile, Zoey replied. "Probably."

"I don't like, 'probably.'" I grumbled to Jill. "I want, 'certainly.'"

Overhearing us yelling to be heard over the roar of the steam, Zoey turned towards us. "I'm almost certain that you'll probably be safe."

"You should be in stand-up comedy," I shouted.

"That's what my fiancé says, too."

After walking over irregular humps and rocks for fifty yards, Zoey stopped. "The scuff marks end here, so this must be where they recovered the body." Pulling two bottles of water from her daypack, Zoey paused. "Stay hydrated. Walking on the dark lava is much hotter than sitting by the pool sipping mai tais."

After taking a few swallows I asked, "How intensively was this area searched?"

"I don't think it was searched at all," Zoey replied. "We thought the victim was a lost hiker, so we recovered his body and that's it."

Although the surface looked like a black rolling meadow, there were large fissures and smaller cracks at the edge of every hump. "Let's circle this spot shoulder to shoulder, checking the depressions and cracks for any of the victim's belongings."

"What are we looking for?" Zoey asked as we spaced ourselves about four feet apart.

"The male victim's car keys are missing, and he was a photographer, so he probably had a camera and a pack with spare lenses and other gear."

"That's it?" Zoey asked.

"We're looking for anything that might've been with the victims. Pick up anything that's not lava."

We were making a second, wider loop when Zoey called out. "I see something." She carefully knelt on the abrasive surface with her bare knees and reached into a crevice. She pulled out a set of smashed headphones with a dangling cord. "Someone must've dropped these out of a tour helicopter."

Jill pointed to the cord. "There's no plug. It looks like they were ripped out of the plugin."

I walked to the women and held open a plastic evidence bag. "Put them in here, please."

Shrugging, Zoey said, "They're probably just junk."

"Over here!" Jill yelled from a few feet away. She knelt down and lifted a camera out of a crevice by its strap. "This isn't some cheap-o camera dropped by an amateur photographer."

Zoey watched Jill's gloved hand drop the camera into an evidence bag. "I've never heard of a Canon 5D Mark II."

"It's probably a high-end camera," I explained, "like a professional photographer would use."

After depositing the camera in the evidence bag, Jill looked around. "There must've been a lens with this."

A minute later, Zoey retrieved the lens from a crack. "I've never seen so many adjustments on a lens," she said as she dropped it into another evidence bag.

An additional fifteen minutes of searching didn't yield the man's keys, or any other human-generated debris.

"Let's check the area where the woman was recovered," I suggested after taking a few more swallows of water.

Zoey pointed toward the hillside. "She was over there."

"Is it safe to walk directly there?" I asked.

Zoey looked toward Jill. "It's no more unsafe than walking here. Will that bother your hemorrhoids?"

"Just go," I replied.

I was about to call off the search when Zoey shouted out. "I've got a cell phone!"

Although it had obviously fallen from a height, the owner had prepared the phone for rough handling. The cushioned case was scraped, but the phone's screen wasn't even cracked.

"We might be able to get data off the sim card," I said as Jill dropped the phone into the evidence bag."

"Yeah," Jill agreed. "This is in a lot better condition than the GPS you recovered from the bottom of the Grand Canyon."

Zoey looked at me with sudden awe. "You investigated someone falling from the Grand Canyon?"

"They went over the rim during a car chase," Jill explained. "Doug's car stopped before it went over."

"Holy shit," Zoey said. "That must've been scary as hell!"

"Not as scary as it was for the occupants of the car that went over the cliff."

"How many survived?" Zoey asked.

"None. The car fell about seven hundred feet."

Zoey looked skyward and I thought she was praying. Nodding, she said, "that would take like 6.6 seconds."

"You just did that calculation in your head?" I asked.

"Yeah, it's a simple kinematic equation for position calculation. You plug in 700 feet for D and…"

"I trust your math."

"I have a double major; physics and math."

"Why aren't you working in the Jet Propulsion Lab or NASA?" I asked as we started back to the pickup.

"Because they're not hiring B.S. math majors *and* they're not in Hawaii. How could I pass up this chance to live in paradise?"

Back in the pickup, Jill asked, "How long have you been stationed in Hawaii?"

After making a U-turn Zoey said, "I've been here eight months."

"What's the best part?" I asked.

"I'm from Colorado and the weather here is always wonderful."

"And the worst?"

Zoey lost her smile. "The Big Island offers some diversity of eating and entertainment. In reality, it's like never leaving the county. I mean, you have to catch a flight to eat at a different restaurant. And everything is expensive, especially on a seasonal ranger's salary."

Jill and Zoey continued the conversation while I examined the camera. "I assume there are fewer tourists during the summer."

"It's not as huge a change here as it is on Maui, which is a big tourist trap. There's less congestion on the roads here, and fewer manic drivers who feel like they have to make the most of their short vacation stay. Most think, "hey, it's just an island," and don't comprehend that it takes a whole day to make a loop from Kailua/Kona to Hilo and back."

"There's no road that cuts across the island?"

"There is Saddleback Road, but I don't think you're supposed to drive rental cars on it. And it's sometimes closed because of snow."

My head popped up. "Snow?"

"Yeah, the altitude is high enough, so we get occasional snow. The schools bring busloads of kids up the volcano to make snowmen and have snowball fights."

"I grew up in South Dakota and six months of snow is not that enticing." Jill looked over her shoulder at me. "Are you making any headway with the camera or phone?"

"The camera is toast. It hit with enough force to break off the lens and crush one corner of the camera body. If I had tools, I think I could pull the memory card. With any luck, we'll be able to access the pictures." I held up the other evidence bag. "The phone is either broken or has a dead battery. We can put it on a charger when we get back."

Jill looked at Zoey. "I don't suppose your boyfriend is a camera or electronics wizard?"

"He's a baker at the banana bread vendor near the black sand beach."

"Bakers start their days very early."

Zoey sighed. "Tell me about it. A late night is him staying up until the prime-time television shows come on at seven o'clock."

* * *

I checked my cell phone when we returned to the visitor center. The message symbol was lit leading me to assume we'd been out of cell phone range while on the lava.

I dialed my voicemail and the electronic voice said I had two messages. "Doug, I may have pissed off a number of people, but someone from the Drug Enforcement Agency will contact you. I'm not sure if they're going to welcome you to the team or tell you to meet them at the Honolulu federal courthouse."

A second message was succinct. "This is DEA Special Agent in Charge Joe Gray. The US Attorney asked me to brief you on an operation. Do not take any further action on the information from your confidential informant before speaking with me."

Jill looked at me as I ended the call. "What's up?"

"I think we just got invited into a DEA investigation."

"Really?"

"Yeah, the special agent in charge told me not to do anything until I spoke with him."

"That doesn't sound like an invitation."

I smiled. "It's the DEA's way of saying. 'Welcome to the team. Don't mess this up or your career will be over.'"

"Are you going to call him back?"

"I'd rather determine Mocha's situation before being ordered not to contact her."

"You're going to ask forgiveness instead of permission."

"Yes."

"One of these times that's not going to end well."

"Someone told me we could retire anytime we wanted to."

"That was before we bought a house next to Matt and Mandy, and I decided that I like this job."

* * *

After a grilled mahi mahi and fried plantain dinner at the Slippery Squid, we returned to the B&B to check out the camera and cell phone we'd found. Jill set up her laptop while I removed the camera's memory card, which was no small feat since everything was bent and misshapen. After several attempts with various blades and screwdrivers on my Leatherman tool, I popped the card from a panel on the camera's edge.

"Can you plug this into your computer?" I asked, holding up the small card.

"My computer has the same slots as yours and you loaded the other memory card." Jill inserted the card into a small slot in her laptop and waited. "Let's hope this works, and the card doesn't have some virus that infects my government computer."

"I think a professional photographer would be very protective of the content on his memory cards."

I sat beside her as she clicked keys to open a photo app. "Wow," she said. "There are hundreds of files."

"Open the most recent file."

Clicking on a .jpg file opened a display of photos. Jill enlarged the last photo, a beautiful shot of the moon over the volcanic steam cloud. "This is incredible," she said. Then her face clouded as she clicked through more images of the moon behind the steam cloud. "These were the last shots taken before the photographer died. They look like they could've been taken from a helicopter."

"Go into the next oldest file."

The pictures showed the ocean surf beating on a black sand beach. Jill looked at me. "Dr. Nakamura said the female victim had black sand ground into her hands and knees. I suppose she crawled on the beach."

"I think she would've brushed the sand off her hands and knees before they left the site. What's the next oldest file?"

A variety of spectacular garden pictures appeared. "I've never seen some of these flowers. They're stunning."

"Click on the .mpg video file," I suggested.

After a second, the video opened with a large group of people socializing around a pool. The crowd was boisterous, the men in long surfer bathing suits, and the women mostly wearing tiny bikinis. "Forty years from now, these people won't want their grandchildren to see them acting like this."

Jill was about to close the video when I stopped her. "Look at the people at the glass-topped table by the hot tub."

Six or seven people huddled around the table, apparently sharing a pipe filled with what I assumed to be some variety of drugs. Laughing and cajoling others to join them, the smokers were feeling no pain. The pipe got passed to the people sitting in the hot tub, then was returned.

"Turn up the volume," I said. "The camera operator is speaking."

Jill pushed the volume arrow. A male voice laughed, then called out to someone. "Jasper, is this the good stuff?"

A dazed man with glassy eyes turned toward the camera. "Yeah, it's better because they add a touch of fentanyl to up the intensity."

Looking away from the scene Jill said, "They're smoking cocaine mixed with fentanyl. That's playing with fire."

"I suspect our colleagues in the DEA will want to see this."

One of the young men stepped out of his bathing suit and cannonballed into the pool, garnering a round of laughter. He invited others to join him as the camera turned to capture the view of naked bodies jumping into the water.

Then there was a scream.

The display was jostled as the cameraman tried to locate the source of the scream. The photographer finally focused on two men lifting an unconscious woman from the hot tub.

One of the women getting out of the hot tub gasped, "I don't think she's breathing."

People scrambled to either see the action, or to gather their things and leave. One of the men who'd carried the woman out of the hot tub laid her on the concrete pool apron and yelled, "Somebody call an ambulance!"

A different male voice yelled, "Nobody panic, she'll be okay. Just put her in my SUV."

The videographer followed as four men carried the unconscious woman through a gate and to a

SUV in the driveway. "I'm blocked in. Get these cars out of the way!"

Jill's hand covered her mouth as we watched the group try to find the cars' owners. Nearly five minutes elapsed before the SUV could leave the driveway. The video ended abruptly after a man's face flashed in front of the camera before the lens was covered by a palm. "Shut that damned thing off and destroy whatever you just recorded."

"Read the timestamp on that video," I said as I started a computer search for a woman who'd died of a drug overdose on the Big Island.

"It's from July fourth of this year."

The search suggested several results. I selected the first one, which was a story from the *Kona Express.* "'A young woman's body was discovered in a condo pool on the morning of July 5th by a maintenance worker. EMTs took her body to the hospital for an autopsy.'"

Jill's fingers were flying over the keyboard as she did her own search. "'Gina Payson, a Hilo flower shop employee, was found dead in a residential condo pool in Kailua on July 5th. The hospital pathologist determined that she died of a drug overdose. South Kona police are investigating, but a spokesperson said it appeared the woman probably died elsewhere, and her body had been dumped in the condo pool. They asked the public to phone in with information.'"

"Rerun the video. I want to take a closer look at the guy who covered the lens. I think I saw him passing the pipe to the people in the hot tub."

After viewing the video again, I called Joe Gray to tell him what we had. Not expecting him to pick up, I was amazed when he said he'd be right over.

Chapter 13

Joe Gray's Hawaiian shirt seemed inappropriate paired with the Drug Enforcement Agency badge hanging from a lanyard. In contrast, Sara McCallie seemed professional in her county police uniform. After introductions, we viewed the deadly party video three times on Jill's laptop.

"I'm convinced the person who covered the camera lens handed the pipe to the woman who was later taken unconscious from the pool. How do we identify him?"

Gray turned and said, "He's known to us."

Jill looked at McCallie. "I think this is sufficient evidence to prove that he's guilty of manslaughter in Gina Payson's death."

McCallie glanced at Gray, then smiled. "Normally, I'd take this to the district attorney, but there's more at play."

"More at play?" Jill asked.

I looked at Gray. "The man is known to you. Is that a euphemism for under surveillance?"

"He's a subject in an active investigation." Gray extended his hand to Jill. "I'd like that memory card. Please erase the video if it's stored in your computer."

Jill leaned back. "We found this evidence as part of our investigation of the Kilauea deaths. I think we'll keep it, for now."

"Officer McCallie is leading that death investigation for the county, and she's seen the video. I suggest that you turn the evidence over to us, and you two can go back to…whatever it is that park rangers do."

I felt Jill's foot nudge mine and saw red creeping up her neck. She was counting on her fingers under the table. I knew things would become ugly if she reached ten before I intervened. "As federal law enforcement officers investigating a death in a national park, we'll retain the video card. We'll gladly load a copy onto a thumb drive for you."

"Ranger Fletcher, have you…"

I cut off Gray's comment. "We're US Park Service Investigators, Agent Gray. If you're unsure of our status, I suggest you contact the director of the USPSIB."

"What's the alphabetic acronym?"

"We work for the US Park Service Investigative Branch. If you do your research, you'll find that we're a federal law enforcement agency, like the DEA, reporting to the Secretary of the Interior. I have no idea what your reporting structure looks like, Agent Gray, but my partner and I are the same grade as an FBI Special Agent in Charge."

Gray stiffened. "Are you trying to pull rank on me?"

"Let's say I'm suggesting that we collaborate on this joint investigation. As part of our federal death investigation, we uncovered evidence that's apparently related to something the DEA is pursuing."

A hint of a grin spread across Jill's face as she closed her computer and pulled it onto her lap. "We showed you ours. It's your turn to show us yours."

Gray motioned for Jill to pass him the computer. "That's not how DEA investigations work, *Investigator Fletcher.*"

Standing, I took a half step back. "Rather than arguing jurisdiction here, I'll have my boss call his Washington counterpart in the DEA. I'm sure they'll figure out how best to deal with our joint interests."

Gray closed his eyes and turned his head. "Jesus, Fletcher. You don't really want to get the bureaucrats involved, do you?"

I placed my hands flat on the table. "We're all cops. We all want to put away bad guys. Let's work on this together."

"People could be killed if there's a leak. I don't want to take that risk."

I removed my ID from my pocket and placed it on the table. "I'm a senior federal law enforcement officer. Are you suggesting that I'd leak your operation?"

"I don't know you two from Adam. There are very few people, *very few*, who are privy to the details of this operation. The risk of a leak grows exponentially when each person is added to the team."

"How close are you to closing the net?" I asked.

"Where did you learn that phrase?"

"I was a St. Paul detective before I joined the Park Service. I worked several joint DEA/SPPD operations. Both my partner and I have been part of arrest teams with the FBI and the US Marshals. We aren't the people you need to keep out of the loop."

Gray clasped his hands as if he was trying to keep from exploding. "There's a federal grand jury considering the evidence we've gathered. Your video could be the one piece that'll get the indictments to kick off the arrests."

I stood. "You're only a day or two from making arrests?"

"We'll have to make plans and assemble teams. But yes, we're only days away from making arrests and seizing a substantial quantity of drugs."

Looking at Jill I asked, "Have you downloaded the video to your computer?"

"Actually, it's saved in the cloud, on a federal server somewhere."

I was about to tell Jill to give the memory card to Gray when the slight taste of shoe leather hit my tongue. "Since you've made a copy, I think we can let Agent Gray have the memory card."

Having been married for nearly two years, Jill sensed my polite rewording of a command. She popped the memory card out of the computer. "I concur," she said as she handed it to Gray. "What's your role in this operation, Officer McCallie?"

The Kona officer stood and smiled. "I've been working as an undercover bartender at a strip club for two years."

Impressed, I said, "Two years is a long time to be undercover."

"It's not all bad. Topless bartenders make really good tips."

I saw Jill's shock as her eyes went to McCallie's chest, then back to her face.

McCallie grinned broadly. "Gotcha. There aren't any topless bars in Hawaii."

Gray chuckled. "It might as well be topless because your short shorts and t-shirt leave little to the imagination."

I was surprised when McCallie batted her eyes and replied in a Southern drawl, "Y'all know there hasn't been a man in that bar who could even tell you what color Blossom's eyes are."

"Blossom?" I asked.

"Yes, sir. I'm Blossom from Toad Suck, Mississippi. I'm an air-headed Southern girl who can barely remember what kind of beer you ordered."

"Won't it be difficult going back into uniform when this is over?" Jill asked.

Switching back to a neutral, almost Midwestern accent, McCallie said, "I'll take some shit from the guys but going to bed at 3 AM is really not my style."

"Every night?" Jill asked.

"It doesn't pay to change the sleep schedule on my days off."

"Do you have a family?"

McCallie nodded. "They're on Kauai. I sometimes get back to see my son play t-ball games in Hanalei."

"We used some women undercover when I was in St. Paul. We'd borrow cops from agencies miles away so their faces wouldn't be familiar to the criminals. Hawaii isn't that big. Aren't you afraid someone will recognize you?"

"I went from blonde to red and I wear long eyelashes. To be honest, not many of the guys are focused on my face when I'm wearing my bar outfit."

Jill glanced at me. "Yeah, men are pigs."

Gray snorted and looked at me. "Aren't you married to Jill, who just said men are pigs?"

"I try to suppress my porcine habits."

McCallie nodded and switched to her Mississippi accent. "You're pretty good. You haven't glanced at Blossom's butt or boobs even once."

Jill sighed. "He's marginally housebroken."

"Marginally?" Gray asked.

"He doesn't stick his foot in his mouth as often as he used to."

Gray raised his eyebrows. "That's a line from my second ex-wife."

"How many have there been?"

"Being the wife of a DEA agent takes a lot of tolerance. Crappy hours. Busts with uncertain outcomes. Dealers with more firepower than us. Depression."

"Alcohol," I added.

Gray blew out a breath. "That's right, you've been there, Fletcher. How many ex-wives do you have?"

"There will only be one," Jill replied before I could answer.

"Only one?" McCallie asked. "As in, you'll kill him before there will be a second divorce?"

Jill's dimples appeared as she smiled at me. "It won't be a murder. Just a 'gun cleaning accident.'"

Gray chuckled. "Tell us about your informant."

"She has inside information about the strip club operation. She knows about the money laundering and where the bodies are buried."

Jill looked at McCallie and added, "And she wants to be off the island before the party with the Asian businessmen this weekend."

Gray cocked his head. "Do you know about an upcoming party, McCallie?"

"The girls have been grumbling about it. They don't like being pimped out to the owner's clients."

Jill tipped her head back. "According to our informant, the Asian clients are poorly behaved."

McCallie had a hard time looking Jill in the eye. "I've only heard the stories…and seen the bruises."

Jill leaned across the table, getting as close to Gray's face as she could. "Those girls should be in protective custody before the party."

Gray looked surprised. "The timing is controlled by the US Attorney's office and the grand jury. I have no control over when they'll get an indictment."

Jill stood. "Agent Gray, is the US Attorney aware of the implications of a delay past this weekend?" When Gray didn't respond, Jill turned to McCallie. "You must have a contact in the US Attorney's office. Let them know what's about to happen if they delay the arrests."

McCallie looked at Agent Gray. "You need to make a call. Those women's lives could be at risk."

Jill nodded. "If you delay past Saturday, your best informant will be gone. She told us that she will 'do whatever she has to' to be off the island before that party."

Gray pinched the bridge of his nose as if he was getting a headache. "I'll call, but I can't guarantee anything."

* * *

I leaned close to Jill after exiting the conference room. "You pushed Gray pretty hard in there."

"Mocha's situation is irrevocable. The DEA either acts now or she'll be gone."

We walked toward the door. "If I divorced you there'd be a gun cleaning accident?"

Without breaking stride, Jill replied, "They happen all the time."

"You just told two cops you'd kill me before you'd divorce me."

Jill bumped me with her shoulder. "I guess you'd better not give me justification."

"My mother would be suspicious," I replied.

"Are you kidding? Your mother would say you'd given me motive. Then, she'd swear that the shooting was an accident."

I shook my head.

Jill smiled and bumped me again. "You know it's true, don't you?"

"How did you get my mother on *your* side?"

"You're joking, right?"

"No. I'd really like to know why she moved from my corner to yours."

"I return her phone calls. You don't."

"That's it? My mother likes you better because you return her calls?"

Exiting the air-conditioned building into the muggy air, our noses were tickled by the stink of sulfur dioxide. "Ronnie loves me because I listen to her concerns and express empathy. I hug her when we meet, and I *do* return her phone calls."

"You win. You're the one who expresses empathy for her ridiculous concerns and answers her medical questions."

"See! I'm the favored child. The daughter she always wished she'd had."

After unlocking its doors with the remote, we climbed into the pickup. "You win. If that's what it takes to win Mom over, she's yours."

"Fletcher! She's your mother. You could make an effort."

I started the engine. "I've got you to cover her needs. I'm good with where I'm at."

"You are a hopeless case."

I leaned across the seat and kissed Jill's cheek. "But I'm *your* hopeless case."

"It's too bad you won't be in heaven with me."

"Are we having the heaven and hell discussion again? St. Jill isn't planning to pull her sinning husband along to heaven on her coattails?"

"I'm afraid the weight will be too great, and you'd pull me down as you sink."

I turned out of the Hilo police station parking lot and turned toward Volcano Village. "I'll tell you what. We'll have a bottle of wine with supper, then we'll see who's the saint and who's the sinner."

"That's low."

"What's the matter, honey? Are you afraid a couple glasses of wine will tarnish the shine on your halo?"

"It was easier to be celibate when I was single and drank alone."

Reaching across the seat, I squeezed Jill's hand. "Isn't marriage better?"

"I heard the Catholic church had a list of one hundred mortal sins, the ones that guarantee a trip to hell. The story is that ninety-seven of the hundred were sexually related."

"Great! We'll have supper with a bottle of wine, then go to the B&B to see how many of the ninety-seven mortal sins we can commit before we fall asleep."

Jill started to laugh.

"What's funny?"

"You're more of a one-trick pony, then asleep kind of guy."

With my ego slightly bruised I replied, "It could happen."

"Wait!" Jill said, looking toward the sky. "Is that a pig flying?"

"Smartass."

She patted my hand. "It's one of my superpowers."

"Really? What's another of your superpowers?"

"It might be one of the ninety-seven mortal sins…"

Intrigued, I said, "Maybe we should skip supper."

"It appears that the DEA plans don't include us. Take me to the Hawaiian shirt shop in Hilo."

Pulling to the side of the road, I stopped. "If you're thinking of buying a swimsuit, I'll give you the car and I'll walk to the B&B."

"We're miles from the B&B."

"Based on history, I'll be back there before you buy a swimsuit even if I walk from here."

"Be a good sport. You can buy a Hawaiian shirt to cover your gun and badge, and a pair of the baggy surfer shorts."

After checking the mirrors, I made a U-turn. "Maybe I'll buy Matt and Mandy matching Hawaiian shirts."

"I don't think that'll work. Mandy is very particular about the clothing she chooses."

I tried to put on my best Cheshire cat grin. "I know. That's why it'll be fun." Pausing, I added. "You could buy a loose-fitting Hawaiian shirt, so your Glock doesn't show."

I could feel the withering glare I was getting without looking toward Jill. "A shirt baggy enough to cover my Glock would make me look like I was wearing a pregnancy smock. A Hawaiian-themed purse or small tote might work better."

"I've seen women try to draw a pistol from a purse, it's not something that happens in a heartbeat."

"I've got news for you, dear. Trying to wrestle a Glock from under a Hawaiian shirt that's halfway to my knees isn't happening quickly, either."

I had an idea as we approached downtown. "Get a fanny pack."

"Think about that. The adjective 'fanny' implies it would be worn behind me. Then, there's the issue of the zipper."

"I'll look for a gun shop that sells Hawaiian print holsters."

"I don't think Hilo is a big enough market to have a gun shop," Jill said as I turned into the parking lot of a small shop advertising locally made shirts and shorts.

"You're probably right. I'll drive over to Kona while you shop for a swimsuit."

"Kona is a three-hour drive."

"No problem. I'll get a cup of coffee to kill time."

"All right, smartass. I get the hint about the time it takes me to choose a swimsuit. However, your hint won't change the issue of finding a tasteful swimsuit that fits me. I'll give you the choice of waiting patiently, or you can wander off and I'll call your cell phone when I'm through."

Looking at the one-block strip mall that appeared to be primarily law offices and realtors I said, "Really? You'll set me free in the metropolis of Hilo all by myself while you look for a swimsuit?"

"Sure. I'll even pick out a Hawaiian shirt and surfer shorts for you."

"Having become an insightful and housebroken husband, I perceive that leaving now would be unwise."

I followed Jill into the shop. "Call your mother while you're waiting for me."

Checking my watch and calculating the time in Rapid City, I realized it was evening. "It's after eight o'clock. They might be in bed."

Jill held up a one-piece bathing suit and considered its look in a mirror. "Perfect. Your mother likes to have heart to heart conversations after Chet goes to bed."

Not realizing that I'd groaned out loud, I was surprised when the shopkeeper rushed over. "Are you okay, sir?"

"I'm fine. Do you have a fishing magazine and a chair I can sit in?"

The woman's eyes sparkled, her grin bringing crow's feet to the corners of her eyes. "The bored husband waiting area is in the back. There's a cooler filled with water bottles and a cabinet with chips. Help yourself."

* * *

Forty-five minutes later I heard Jill speaking with the shop owner, so I set the *Honolulu Advisor* aside and walked to the front of the store. The shopkeeper was clipping off tags as she rang up a pile of clothing and placed the pieces into a canvas shopping tote.

"They give you a canvas tote when you shop here?" I asked.

"Are you kidding?" Jill replied as she pulled a credit card from her back pocket. "I thought a pretty shopping bag with a plumeria flower on it would be a nice Hawaiian souvenir."

"Buy two more and we can give them to our mothers for Christmas."

"Good thought. They're on the rack by the door. Get three more."

I was lifting bags off a peg when the question struck me. "Why do we need three more? There are only two mothers."

"I'm keeping this tote. The others are for Mandy and our mothers."

Grumbling, I carried the totes to the cash register. "Do you plan to carry your Glock in a giant canvas tote?"

The shopkeeper paused and handed Jill a small handbag that appeared to have been crafted from grass reeds and the cloth from a Hawaiian shirt. "Her Glock fits nicely in this bag. There's a thin leather strap inside that can go over her shoulder if she wants her hands free to shoot."

"Really? You and this nice woman discussed your Glock at some length?"

The shopkeeper smiled. "My husband retired from Immigration and Customs Enforcement. I'm accustomed to having a gun-toting man in the house."

Jill emptied tissue paper from the small bag, pulled her Glock out of its holster, and slipped it inside. Closing the bag with a Velcro strap she smiled. "See. It fits perfectly."

Jill's bathing suit went into the shopping bag and the shopkeeper totalled the transaction. Seeing the surprise on my face at the over $1,000 total, the shopkeeper smiled. "I gave Jill the law enforcement discount."

"Um…thanks."

The shopkeeper handed me two shopping bags, then she hugged Jill. "*Mahalo*. It's been a slow week."

"A thousand dollars?" I whispered after the door closed behind us.

"Doug, her husband is disabled after being shot by a drug smuggler during a bust. The shop is *getting by* but they're not getting rich. We're only the second customers she's had today. All the products are made by local artisans. Everything I bought, I wanted. And we can afford it." Jill paused as I loaded the bags into the pickup. "Do you have any other criticisms that I can knock down?"

I pulled Jill into a hug and kissed her forehead. "I love you."

She looked up at me as the fire faded from her eyes. "Good answer."

"It looks like there's a sushi shop at the end of the block. It sounds tempting."

After staring at her shoes for a second, Jill replied. "I don't think they put any raw fish into a California roll, so sushi will be okay."

I clicked the fob to lock the pickup's doors. "We've never discussed eating raw fish when we were dating."

"Trout are a Black Hills thing, but we never eat them raw. I've eaten catfish, crawdads, fish and chips, and tilapia, all of them cooked. The thought of putting a raw fish in my mouth gags me."

"But you've eaten liver, antelope, and rocky mountain oysters."

"They were all cooked and as I said before, I don't intend to eat any of them again in this lifetime."

"I think they have nigiri with cooked shrimp on top."

We stood outside the sushi restaurant, studying the menu as an Asian couple walked in. "I could try the shrimp nigiri if they promised not to slip any unagi into it."

"Unagi?"

Jill shuddered. "Unagi is eel."

"We could eat somewhere else."

Jill opened the door. "I think a California roll with cucumber, rice, and avocado sounds good." We stopped at the counter. "What are you having?"

"Spicy ahi rolls sound good."

At the counter we ordered sushi and a pot of jasmine tea. We chose a small table in the back of the dining area where I could face the door. Jill leaned close, as if she had a thought about the case. "You do realize that I will not kiss you with the smell of raw tuna on your breath, nor will I hold your head while you suffer through food poisoning."

"This is an established shop. They'd be out of business if their customers had food poisoning."

"Didn't you read the warning about consuming raw or undercooked fish?"

"It must've been in Japanese."

A pre-teen waiter, no doubt part of the owner's family, delivered a teapot and two small cups. "Enjoy!" he said in unaccented English.

"How long has your family owned this shop?" I asked.

"My dad's the third generation of sushi chefs. He's teaching me."

"Has the restaurant always been in this location?"

The boy pointed out the front window. "Do you see the palm tree with the metal markers across the street?"

"Sure. I was wondering what they were."

"Those are the high-water markers from the tsunamis that have hit Hilo Bay. This building was destroyed by the 1960 tsunami."

"The water was this high?"

The sushi chef delivered our meals. Having overheard the discussion, he nodded. "This is paradise—if you aren't killed by the tsunamis, vog, or lava flows. Enjoy your meals."

After the father walked away, the boy leaned close. "Head for higher land if you hear the Civil Defense sirens."

Setting aside the chopsticks, Jill picked up a California roll in her fingers, dipped it in soy sauce, then popped it into her mouth. "How high do you think we need to go if we hear the sirens?"

"How do we know if the threat is tsunami, vog, or a lava flow if the sirens go off?" I asked.

Wiping her fingers on a napkin, Jill pulled her phone out of her new bag and set it on the table. "I downloaded the Hawaii Civil Defense app when we arrived. I'll get a warning message if there's an alert."

"I find this all very unsettling," I said as a piece of sushi slipped from my chopsticks and rolled onto the table.

"You lived in 'tornado alley' most of your life, then you moved to the hurricane coast of Texas, and you find Hawaiian threats unsettling?"

Picturing a map of the U.S. in my head, I tried to envision an area that was exempt from natural disasters, as I tried to retrieve the sushi with the chopsticks. "Maybe we should move to Arizona."

"Which part? Do you want to be up north where they have blizzards and wildfires, or down south where there's no water and temperatures are over 110°F during the summer?"

Giving up on the chopsticks, I picked up the sushi with my fingers and popped it into my mouth. "Okay, where could we move so that there aren't any natural disasters?"

"The Black Hills are pretty nice."

Sighing, I shook my head. "I left myself open for that shot, didn't I?"

"Speaking of shots, do you think DEA Agent Gray is going to invite us along when they execute their warrants?"

"Why would you want to..." I paused. "You've turned into an adrenaline junkie."

"It's not that. I just feel like we've been part of his case. I'd like to be on hand for the finale." Jill pushed her plate aside and took out a business card. She punched a number into her phone and waited. "Hi, Joe. This is Jill Fletcher. We'd like to participate when the end comes."

After a couple of "Uh huhs," Jill closed the phone.

"Did he politely tell you to go back to ticketing litterers while the big boys took care of real police business?"

Jill put the phone into her bag without speaking, then looked at the people sitting at the tables around us. "Later."

"Really?" I asked.

Jill nodded and pulled her plate back in front of her. She sprinkled soy sauce on her California roll and stared at me. "He may have a job for us. We can discuss the details later."

As we walked to the pickup I asked, "What did Gray say?"

Jill glanced at a couple who'd walked out behind us, then waited to reply until we were in the pickup and on the road. "The grand jury issued sealed indictments this afternoon and Gray's team has been strategizing how to execute the arrests while minimizing the risk of injury to his team or civilians. During a break, Gray showed his boss the party video and explained the need to make the arrests before the weekend. When the team reconvened, the boss asked Gray to show everyone the video. The agents in attendance identified about a third of the partygoers."

"Did they invite us along for the arrests?"

"He asked us to meet him tomorrow morning at the Hilo police station."

"Why?"

"He didn't say."

"I see a liquor store ahead. Do you want red or white wine?"

"Your breath smells like a day-old tuna can."

"What?"

"Your breath stinks of tuna from the sushi. I don't see romance in your short-term future."

"I'll brush my teeth."

"I think it's oozing out of your pores."

"I'm sure...."

"Stop breathing on me."

"I'm not even facing you."

Jill rolled down her window. "Face away from me when you exhale."

"You're being overly dramatic."

"I checked your horoscope. It says *put off romance for a different night*."

"It can't be any worse than when I had anchovies on my Caesar salad."

"Did that night involve romance? I don't think so." She paused. "I might let you sleep in the bed if you brush your teeth and face away from me."

"I can't believe that a little tuna would..."

Jill pushed my chin toward the opposite window. "Believe."

Chapter 14

Agent Gray, the Hawaiian South Kona police chief, and a middle-aged Asian woman I didn't recognize, were drinking coffee in a conference room when we arrived. Gray pulled out the chair next to him for Jill and I sat next to the woman, who nodded to me.

She slid two sheets of paper out of her portfolio, handing one each to Jill and me. "Joe says you're trustworthy."

I scanned the schedule outlined on the sheet, as I answered. "We're senior federal law enforcement officers. I hope that speaks for itself."

Looking unhappy but curious, Jill said, "And you are?"

"I'm the DEA Acting Agent in Charge Akai, from the Honolulu office."

Continuing to read, I said, "It appears you're executing the warrants from the grand jury indictments." Running my finger down the page I read, "While it appears the DEA, local police, and US Marshals will be busy. I don't see any mention of the Park Service."

"We'd like to use you in a different capacity."

I set the paper down. "I'm all ears."

Akai nodded to Gray. After drawing a breath, he said, "We have a problem that you can solve. The man you saw handing out drugs in the party video is Gil Jackson, a helicopter pilot who offers chartered flights. We think he was probably piloting the helicopter when the two victims found on the lava flow either fell, or were pushed, from it. Our phone taps and surveillance have identified him as the main inter-island drug smuggler for the Atocha drug cartel."

"How does that affect us?" Jill asked.

"Mr. Jackson needs to be indisposed while we make the arrests and execute the search warrants."

The police chief cleared his throat. "Ironically, Gil has been very generous with his time, assisting with search operations and rescuing injured hikers. Because of that, he knows nearly every cop on all the islands. He's also assisted the Coast Guard with some drug interdiction operations, so he's also met a number of federal agents from the FBI and DEA."

"You'll have to take him by surprise," I said.

Gray shook his head. "He runs his operation from a remote hangar on a private airfield surrounded by pasture. It's impossible to approach without him seeing us. And we believe he's got a drug shipment ready for distribution inside the hangar."

"How does that affect us?" I asked.

"A confidential informant told us that the drugs are wired to burn if he signals the triggering device that he carries all the time." Gray looked at his boss, who nodded. "You two are unknown to Gil. We'd like you to charter a flight to the opposite side of the island while we raid his hangar."

I leaned back in the chair and stared at the ceiling. "You want Jill and me to get into a helicopter with a drug smuggler to keep him occupied while you raid his hangar and disable an incendiary device before it burns up all your evidence."

Before they could respond to my sarcasm, Jill said, "We'll do it."

To her credit, Acting Agent in Charge Akai was quick enough to grab the arm of my chair before it tipped over. I'd been so focused on framing my refusal that I'd arched my back too quickly, nearly flipping the chair.

Akai laughed. "I take it you disagree with your partner?"

"Geez, Jill. This guy has nothing to lose. We could be killed."

Gray leaned his forearms on the tabletop. "You could say that about any member of our entry teams. All of us are literally putting our lives on the line, while going up against heavily armed drug dealers and distributors."

"But none of you are at risk of crashing into a mountain!"

Fixing me with her glare, Jill said, "What's the plan?"

Akai let go of my chair and faced Jill. "The Volcanoes National Park Superintendent has booked a photographic tour for two of the people from the National Park Service public relations group. He said you're going to photograph the Chain of Craters Road, the Kilauea lava flow, and

227

the recent lava flows outside Volcano Village. You'll be on the backside of Mauna Loa while you're over Volcano Village. That's when we'll hit the hangar."

"Wait! Just because we're on the backside of the mountain doesn't mean this idiot can't trigger the inferno by phone."

"Our informant says he's set up a triggering device that requires line of sight between the trigger and the detonator." Gray paused a beat. "Our team will get in, defuse the detonator, and get out. By the time you return, our team will be inside the hangar and out of sight. When he lands, we'll arrest him, and you'll have had an incredible tour of the island."

"Every battle plan goes to hell when the first shot is fired," I replied.

"What?" Akai asked.

"It's a quote from George Patton. Like the military, we put together our best plan. We all know that the plans can change as soon as a suspect isn't where we think he is, a girlfriend screams, a neighbor sees our people moving into place and calls the suspect, or until we're shot at. Then everything goes to hell."

"Hey," Akai said, "we put together the best plan, based on the best intelligence."

"You won't be the one in the helicopter being piloted by a drug smuggler."

"What time is our tour?" Jill asked.

Checking her watch, Akai replied, "You'll have just enough time to get there for your pre-flight briefing if you leave now."

Jill looked at me, then at Gray. "We need to extract our informant."

Gray shook his head. "No. We can't risk the whole operation by tipping off your informant."

"But…"

Jill was cut off by Akai. "The arrests will disrupt everything. All the kingpins will be fleeing. They won't have time to sweep up the little people."

Jill wasn't pleased but nodded. "Can you at least put someone at their house to make sure one of the suspects doesn't do a drive-by shooting?"

Gray laid his hands flat on the table. "We're not doing anything that would tip off the suspects that there's something going on. Putting someone at your informant's house would be too obvious. Besides, there are dozens of agents on the island already. Having a strange face sitting in a car on an obscure road would signal the smugglers that something was wrong."

"But there are tourists all over," Jill argued. "Your surveillance could look like a lost tourist."

"I don't have any spare people to put on surveillance," Gray countered. "Everyone I brought in has an assignment."

Cutting off further argument I said, "We don't even have a camera."

Gray slid a set of keys across the table to me. "There's a well-used camera bag with two cameras in the back seat of the blue rental car in the lot."

Akai turned to me. "There's one other thing. Park Service photographers don't carry badges and sidearms. Doug, that Sig under your Hawaiian shirt has to go."

"No. No. No." I said, "We're not going unarmed into a helicopter with a drug dealer. That's a deal breaker."

Jill patted her new bag. "I have a Glock. We're good."

* * *

Five minutes later, we were driving toward Waimea in the northern, agricultural portion of the big island. Jill was nervous and fidgeting. "I think we should stop at the strip club and tell Mocha to hide."

"No way. This DEA operation is huge and tipping off Mocha might upset the whole thing."

"But she's scared and at risk."

"There's a possibility that she's part of the ring. She could be using us."

"Mocha is very sincere. I'm sure she's a victim."

"Have you ever heard of Stockholm syndrome?" I asked.

"That's the situation where the kidnapped people become so connected to their kidnappers that they defend them."

"Something like that," I replied. "Mocha may have started out as Jackson's victim, but he's set her up as the owner of the club and she's laundering money for him. She may be a victim *and* a part of the operation. She may be using us as a test, to see if there's a sting coming so she can tip them off."

"Just drive to the club. I'll run in and tell her that she'll be taken care of."

230

I laughed. "Do you have any idea how much you'd stand out in a strip club? The whole place is full of men and strippers. There are no women there in Hawaiian casual dress."

I drove north in silence. Jill was disgusted that I wouldn't warn Mocha, and I didn't want to scratch that scab. We were passing through the tiny town of Hakalau when Jill finally spoke. "I'm kind of excited about the helicopter ride."

"I dislike helicopters even more than I dislike horses."

"That's because you're a control freak," Jill replied. "You aren't the helicopter pilot, so you feel like your life is in someone else's hands."

"My life *is* in someone else's hands."

"I've only ridden in a helicopter once. I was in a Border Patrol helicopter searching for lost hikers when I was in Big Bend National Park."

"I had enough helicopter rides for a lifetime when I was in the National Guard. We had an engine failure and the pilot had to auto rotate for a jarring landing."

"But you survived," Jill said, trying to sound upbeat.

"I walked away. Correction, we sat in the middle of the desert baking our brains until they sent another helicopter to rescue us."

"I think this will be fun."

I glanced at Jill. "I hope you still feel that way tomorrow." I paused. "Call my mother."

"Why?"

"Because I want you to explain that this was your idea. She yells at me when she thinks I put you in danger."

Jill didn't reach for her phone.

"What's wrong?"

"Let's tell her afterwards. We can all laugh about it."

Chapter 15

The turn for the Waimea heliport was unmarked except for a pair of mailboxes. Jill advised me of the upcoming turn based on the routing app in her cell phone. "This road isn't even on the car rental map."

"I assume that means that the company doesn't want their cars driven down here."

"Um…the forbidden roads are marked in red, like the route to the observatory. It's more like this is a driveway."

Barbed wire fences lined both sides of the road and a few cattle grazed in the lush green pasture. "My dad and Uncle Chet would kill to have pastures this thick and green. They can probably graze one or two cattle to an acre here."

Intrigued by that statistic, I asked, "How many cattle an acre does your ranch support?"

"We figure thirty acres per steer."

"Thirty acres per steer?"

"That was what killed off all the small homesteads that were established by the original Black Hills settlers. They all came from out east; Indiana, Illinois, and Ohio, where the gulf stream carries moisture north and they have nice green pastures. They arrived in the Black Hills to homestead 160 acres, assuming they'd be able to raise a small herd of milk cows. The reality was that there's so little water, raising dairy cattle was impossible. If they were lucky enough to have water, they were able to raise a half dozen head of beef cattle, and that wasn't enough to sustain the family. Ultimately, the small homesteads were consolidated into larger and larger ranches until there was enough acreage to make a living."

"I see two helicopters ahead of us," I said as we passed a small stand of trees.

The helicopters sat next to a hangar large enough to house the two helicopters and whatever maintenance and support equipment they required. A slender man wearing green coveralls emerged from what appeared to be an office door as we rolled to a stop.

Unlike everyone else we'd encountered, this man seemed less than pleased to see us. "Are you the Park Service photographers or are you lost?"

Jill approached the man while I took the camera bag out of the back seat. "We're the photojournalists," Jill said, extending her hand. "I'm Jill and my partner is Doug."

"Gil Jackson." Reluctantly, the man shook her hand. "You're late, and I slipped you into an opening I made after my arm was twisted."

Jill poured out her charm, soothing the man's anger. "My mapping app didn't believe there was a road here. I'm so sorry. It's all my fault."

Assessing the scarred camera bag as I approached, the man apparently accepted Jill's explanation. "Come inside the office. I'll give you the abbreviated version of the mandatory FAA briefing." He looked over his shoulder. "Have either of you ever ridden in a helicopter before?"

"I had a few trips, courtesy of the Minnesota National Guard," I replied.

"And I shot some pictures over Big Bend National Park a few years ago," Jill explained.

Nodding, the man led us to a set of four chairs arranged facing a wall covered with posters. He leaned against the only desk. "Here are the basics: Stay in your seats, don't unbuckle your seatbelts, wear the headphones all the time because it's noisy, talk to me over the voice-activated intercom, and don't touch any of the controls. Got it?"

We nodded.

"There are airsick bags in the seatbacks. Use them if you feel queasy. If you blow your lunch, I'll give you a sponge and bucket to clean up when we return."

"Where are the headphones?" Jill asked.

"They're hanging from overhead brackets." When we didn't have any further questions, he stood. "I assume you want the door open, so you don't have to shoot through a hazy window."

A vision of flying in the military helicopter while carrying an M-16 and wearing a vest with a dozen magazines flashed through my mind. The Army pilot had shouted we were taking fire. Moments later, the engine sputtered. I heard the pilot shouting MAYDAY into his headset as the helicopter engine sputtered again and stopped.

Jill's hand on my arm jarred me back. "Are you ready to go?"

I felt a trickle of sweat run down my neck. "Yeah. Let's do it."

Gil stood next to the helicopter, ready to help Jill step into the cabin. I followed, taking the seat nearest to the open door. As Gil circled around to the pilot's door, Jill rubbed her fingers and held them out to me. "There's coarse black sand on the floor under your seat."

I leaned close to her and whispered as I buckled my seatbelt. "We'll collect some and put it in evidence bags after we return." We donned the headsets, and I took a camera out of the bag and put the strap around my neck.

Gil was a skilled pilot, easing the helicopter off the ground and slowly ascending as he turned south. Taking pictures as we passed the Mauna Loa observatory, I spoke into the microphone mounted on the headset. "Are we going to fly over the Kona coffee district?"

"If you want to get some pictures there, we should do it on the trip south. The clouds move in every afternoon, which is why Kona coffee is so unique. The clouds protect the coffee cherries from the afternoon sun, so they ripen slowly, making the coffee more mellow than the coffee grown in Kauai, Kenya, and Colombia."

"That's what justifies the $40 per pound price?" Jill asked.

"To tell the truth, I drink coffee for the caffeine, not the mellow flavor," Gil replied. "One of the growers said coffee heathens like me drink coffee made from the crappy second quality beans they sell to the big companies. The alternative would be to use those beans as fertilizer."

"He sounds a bit arrogant," I said.

"If you believe the Kona Coffee Grower's Co-op literature, they have every right to be arrogant. There are specific limits on the geography and altitude of what can be classified as Kona coffee. If you go to their tasting rooms, they'll let you taste samples of their very best coffees. They are mellow. But, like I said, I'm more interested in the caffeine than the mellowness of the coffee." Gil slowed the helicopter as we passed a hillside covered with thousands of small trees. "Here's the Kona coffee district. Snap your photos."

Jill checked her watch as we turned south, gaining speed. She nodded to me, indicating that the DEA and US Marshals should be executing their warrants.

"Hey, Gil, we're running a little behind. Can we zip over to the lava fields and Volcano Village?" I asked.

I was pushed gently back into my seat as Gil accelerated and turned east. The southern coastline of the big island came into view, followed by the view of the ocean beyond.

I felt the vibration of my cell phone, the ringer drowned out by the thumping of the helicopter. Assuming it was my mother, I ignored the call and let it roll over to voicemail. A minute later, Jill reacted to her vibrating phone. She slid the headphones to her left ear and listened to the caller. I saw her momentary look of surprise before she handed the phone to me.

Pulling off the headphones, I took Jill's phone. The male voice was drowned out by the thumping helicopter and wind rushing past the open door. Gil glanced at me, appearing irritated. The only word I thought I'd heard was booby-trapped. I jammed my finger into my left ear and pressed the phone hard against my right ear. "We're in the helicopter, approaching the lava flow. You have to speak up."

"The whole hanger is booby-trapped. Our bomb guy is working on the triggers, but it's going to take him a while to disarm them. He says the main charge is phone-activated. You have to keep Jackson off his phone, or we'll be cooked."

I processed the information as Jackson watched me over his shoulder. Thinking fast, I nodded. "I'm a professional! Of course, we'll shoot the Chain of Craters Road. You didn't need to call and remind me." I punched the phone angrily, ending the call.

Jill accepted the phone and slid it into her bag, leaving it open so I could see the butt of her Glock.

I put the headphones back and tried to sound disgusted. "The boss wants to make sure we get shots of the Chain of Craters. How far away is that?"

Jackson looked out the Plexiglass window. "We're maybe five minutes away. It's on the way to the lava flow." He glanced at the dashboard clock. "If we spend much time there, we won't have time to get pictures of Volcano Village."

"Charge us whatever you have to. We need to get photos of the Chain of Craters, the Kilauea lava flow, and Volcano Village."

"It's not the money. I have to be back to refuel for a noon charter."

"Screw your noon charter. The Park Service is a big customer, and we need pictures of Volcano Village. We'll cover whatever it costs to make things right with your other charter."

"Are you serious? The Park Service charter barely covers my fuel and maintenance cost. The only reason I accept your charters is to fill downtime."

Having no idea how much time the bomb disposal expert needed, I grasped for a straw. "I've got a Park Service credit card in my pocket. Charge whatever you think is fair to give us another fifteen minutes."

Jackson stared ahead, apparently considering what I'd offered. "Fine. It'll cost you three grand for another fifteen minutes."

He glanced at me, and I was sure he expected me to refuse or negotiate. "Do it! Just get me enough time over the three locations to get some decent shots, and you can make it five grand."

The helicopter rotated slightly to the left as Jackson slowed our speed. "Start shooting. That's the Chain of Craters Road below us."

Turning in my seat, I aimed the camera at the road winding through a string of volcanic craters dating back through the twentieth century. I held the shutter release and felt, as much as heard, the camera clicking off a series of photos and we drifted slowly above the roadway. A group of tourists on a raised platform near the end of the trail waved as we passed overhead.

"Make another pass over the smiling and waving crowd."

Jackson's quick loop pushed my stomach into my throat. Breathing deeply to suppress my wave of nausea, I put the camera to my eye as we hovered over the waving tourists.

"Won't you need releases from those people before you can publish those photos?" Jackson asked.

"We're high enough that their faces aren't recognizable," I said, hoping that was a legitimate comment.

"That's the Kilauea lava flow ahead of us. It must be slowing because the laze cloud isn't as big."

"It was bigger earlier?" Jill asked.

"Yeah, a few days ago it was huge. Right before the wind changed..."

"When was that?" Jill asked as I pretended to take pictures of the steam cloud.

"It was...on the news. I think it peaked about Wednesday." The helicopter turned after making a pass close to the steam. "Did you get enough here? Can we move on to Volcano Village?"

"I'd like to get another series of the steam from a lower altitude," I said, trying to delay our trip as long as possible.

Jackson made a loop, then hovered with the steam cloud visible through the open door.

"Can you go lower?" I asked.

"The Park Service regulations restrict me to this altitude or higher. You should know that if..."

I continued to take pictures, but my skin tingled, much like the times I was listening to someone lying about the circumstances of a crime.

"We're done." Jackson said, turning the helicopter away from the ocean and gaining altitude.

"We need Volcano Village," Jill protested.

The helicopter's acceleration pushed us into our seats as Jackson sped up and gained altitude. We were about to crest the hills behind the lava flow when Jackson's phone buzzed loud enough to be heard over the roar of the engine and rushing wind. Jill looked at me, her eyes questioning our next move.

Jackson's seat was more than three feet away from me, well out of my reach. He had an urgent discussion with someone, then ended the call. With one hand on the controls, he was about to start punching a number into the phone when I unbuckled my seatbelt, leaned forward, and swatted the phone out of his hand. It clattered to the floor.

The look he gave me over his shoulder was almost feral. "Are you guys DEA or Marshals?"

Jill spoke into the microphone. "We're Park Service photographers."

"Bullshit. The DEA is all over my hangar. My mechanic just called."

Kneeling next to Jackson, I spoke into the intercom. "It's over, Gil. Just set the helicopter down next to the Park Service visitor center and we'll have someone pick you up."

I heard his phone ring on the floor. Luckily, it was out of his reach. He glanced down. "That code tells everyone that they're on their own. The DEA must be making a raid."

"It's okay. Just set us down somewhere. Anywhere. We can all walk away."

"Shit. Shit. Shit. I've got to get to Lanai. I can grab a boat…"

"You can't get away, Gil. You haven't got the range to get anywhere but another island, and the Coast Guard is shutting down all the boat traffic. It's over. Just set it down."

"I'm dead. I mean, dead, dead. If the inventory is…"

"There's a bomb expert defusing your booby traps and the DEA is loading the inventory into trucks. It's over."

"I'm not going to jail…"

The helicopter veered hard right and gained altitude. The move tossed me against Jill, then it nearly threw me out of the open door. I grabbed my seat with both hands and legs, trying to hold on while the helicopter made wild gyrations.

I felt, as much as I saw, Jill pull the Glock from her bag. "Set the helicopter down," she ordered.

"You are nuts!" Jackson laughed. "You're going to shoot the one person who can land this safely. Really?"

"Doug was a helicopter pilot in Iraq. I shoot you, and he lands the helicopter."

Hearing the exchange between Jill and Jackson almost made me scream. I looked at Jill and gave the slightest headshake, hoping she'd catch the hint that not only didn't I know how to land a helicopter, we'd be unable to wrestle Jackson out of the seat with the helicopter spinning out of control.

She wasn't deterred. Pressing the Glock's muzzle against the back of Jackson's head, Jill repeated her order. "Land the helicopter."

Jackson's laugh echoed over the intercom.

Lacking any plan that would get us down safely, I tried one gambit. With my legs clamped around my seat, I reached past Jill's feet. With one hand on the base of the pilot's seat, I grabbed the bottom of the cyclic, the control held in the pilot's right hand, to adjust the helicopter's tilt. I pulled, causing the helicopter to lurch hard to the right, pressing me against Jill's legs and away from the open door.

"What the hell are you doing?" Jackson screamed as he struggled to regain control.

Jerked by the sudden movement, Jill's body was thrown left, banging her arm against the frame, and knocking the gun out of her hand. Jackson overcompensated, and jerked the cyclic control the opposite way, flopping us to the right.

Holding onto the base of the pilot's seat with my hands, and keeping my legs squeezing my own seat, I was barely able to overcome the gravitational pull toward the open door as the helicopter veered to the left. Jill's Glock rattled around the passenger compartment like a ping pong ball, bouncing off the ceiling, seats, windshield and the pilot's head before coming to rest at her feet.

Obviously rattled, Jackson swore. "ARE YOU TRYING TO KILL US?"

I tried to modulate my voice to lower the threat. "Easy, Gil. Nobody is trying to kill anyone."

Jill was less controlled, "You idiot! You're trying to kill us all, and you're yelling at Doug because he jerked the controls!"

The Glock slid against my legs as Jackson leveled the helicopter. Letting go of the pilot's seat with my left hand, I grabbed the Glock and fumbled with it to get my hand around the gun's butt. In my head, I heard the voice of my first pistol range officer saying, "Only idiots wave their guns around, threatening to shoot someone. If you're in a shooting situation, don't threaten, pull the trigger."

All I could see of Jackson were his calves under the seat. I pointed the Glock at his left calf and pulled the trigger.

Although the helicopter and wind noise were loud, the sound of the Glock firing inside the passenger compartment was deafening. The bullet passed through the pilot's calf, shattering the Plexiglass in the door. Jackson's howl over the intercom was chilling.

The helicopter pitched forward, and we accelerated downward, pushing me away from the pilot. I handed Jill the Glock and used the momentum to flop myself back into my seat where I buckled my seatbelt.

Jackson swore as the helicopter started a slow counter clockwise spin. "I've lost control of the tail rotor. Your shot severed a control cable."

Jill's look of terror mirrored my own feelings. She handed me the Glock. "Do something."

I wrapped my left arm around her shoulder and pulled her close. "Our lives are in God's hands."

The three-minute downward spiral ended with a jarring crash that banged us against each other as the helicopter's left side slammed into a lava outcropping. Reacting totally on instinct, I released my seatbelt which made me fall against Jill. Her forehead was covered with blood oozing from a cut above her hairline, and her eyes were closed.

"Can you get free?" I asked.

Her eyes flickered open. With blood flowing into them, she asked, "Are we in the same place?"

"We are. We're still in the helicopter," I replied, assuming she was disoriented from the blow to her head. I unbuckled her seatbelt and pulled her arms around my neck. "Hang onto me."

"Where are you taking me?" she asked as she clutched me.

"Away from here."

After climbing out of the smoldering helicopter, I wiped the blood from Jill's forehead, trying to discern the location and severity of her injuries. She wiped the blood away from her own eyes, then looked at the black lava field, extending as far as we could see around us. The sulphurous stink of the vog intermingled with the smell of smoldering plastic and fuel. "Damn. It looks like you won," she said.

I stripped off my shirt and pressed it to the oozing cut on her head. "What did I win?"

"This is hell, isn't it?"

Finally understanding her comments, I started to laugh. "This isn't hell. We're in paradise."

"If this isn't hell, why is it so hot and stinky, and why is everything black?"

"The helicopter crashed into a lava field. We're alive."

"The helicopter?"

"We were in a helicopter and..." Making the assessment that Jill was confused, but apparently suffering only from a concussion, I realized that Gil hadn't exited the helicopter. I laid Jill down on her back, then jogged back into the helicopter wreckage. Due to the rotation of the helicopter, the impact flipped the wreckage, with it coming to rest on the left/pilot's side.

Climbing through the open passenger door, I lowered myself into the fuselage. Jackson was slumped at the controls, his body straining against the seat belt with his head resting against the shattered left door. I put my fingers on his neck but couldn't feel a pulse. "Gil, can you hear me?"

A whoosh signaled ignition of the leaking fuel. With flames licking at my arms and legs, I struggled to climb across the seats to the passenger door. I covered my face with my hands as I jumped from the passenger compartment and tumbled through the fire onto the black lava. I rolled, my arms, legs, and hands burning, hoping that I'd rolled free of the flames.

I ran to Jill, who was attempting to push herself upright. Lifting her, I moved her farther from the inferno of the burning helicopter.

"Are you sure this isn't hell? I smell burning hair."

I hugged her tight. "With any luck, we've just passed through purgatory on our way to heaven."

Still dazed, she tried to focus on my face. "Have you read Dante's *Inferno*?"

"We didn't read the classics..." I stopped, realizing I was trying to explain my high school reading list to a woman who had a concussion and was probably in shock. "Just lie down."

"Don't you smell the burning sulfur?"

"It's the vog," I said as I patted my pockets, hoping to find my cell phone, and hoping it was undamaged. I punched in 911. "Dispatcher, I'm Douglas Fletcher from the US National Park Service. We've been in a helicopter crash."

"Where are you, Mr. Fletcher?"

I looked around, trying to identify a landmark in the barren black lava field. A distant road cut through the lava field, where a red pickup had stopped. Two men were scrambling across the rough lava as a black plume rose from the burning helicopter.

"I don't know, but I'm sure there have been a half dozen calls about the black smoke plume. I'm sitting next to the helicopter with a second injured passenger."

"Were you the pilot?"

I looked at the crash wreckage. What had been a smoldering fire was now a raging blaze fed by the leaking fuel. "No, he died in the crash."

"Mocha," Jill uttered.

"I'm sure she's fine."

"We need to…"

"You need to go to the hospital."

In the distance, a siren wailed.

Chapter 16

After being stripped naked, poked, prodded, and x-rayed, I sat alone in the ER exam room wearing a hospital gown. My arms, face, torso and legs were smeared with Silvadene to treat the second-degree burns I'd received while trying to rescue the pilot.

I wondered what was happening to Jill. We'd been delivered to the hospital in the same ambulance, me sitting on a jump seat and Jill lying on the gurney. She'd had a conversation with the EMT on the drive. Having seen numerous car accident victims, I understood that the EMT's conversation was actually an assessment of Jill's mental faculties. "What's your name? What day is it? Who's the president?" She'd breezed through those questions, but stumbled on where she was, stuck with the impression she was dead and now in hell.

Ignoring the NO CELL PHONE sign in the exam room, I dug my shorts out of the plastic hospital bag and pulled out the cell phone. Happy to see the battery had more than 50% of the charge left, and that I had two bars of service, I selected Jack Pardee's phone number from my contacts and hit the *call* button.

"Pardee speaking."

"Hi, Jack. I thought I should call you before you read about the deadly tourist helicopter crash on the Big Island."

"Um, thanks. Why would I care about the crash of a tourist helicopter?"

"Jill and I were onboard when it went down."

I heard a creak that I assumed was Jack sitting up in his chair. "What were you doing on a helicopter?"

"The DEA needed a couple of unrecognizable faces for an undercover operation." I paused. "I'll also have to file a report on the discharge of my duty weapon. Actually, I discharged Jill's weapon."

"I appreciate the update, but could you back up a bit? The last I heard, you were concerned about a woman in the house next to the B&B. Was your crash related to that?"

Closing my eyes, I thought back and explained the activities of the previous two days to Jack. "Jill bumped her head when we crashed, and she probably has a concussion. She's in a separate exam room."

"You're in the hospital? Now?"

"I probably should've prefaced our discussion with that information."

"Hell yes, Doug. Jill has a concussion. How are you?"

"Bruised but unbroken."

"I'm making notes for a call to my boss. Repeat the part where you shot the helicopter pilot."

"He told us he was going to be killed by the drug cartel, so his plan was to crash the helicopter and kill all three of us."

"And you thought shooting the pilot was a better option than him just crashing the helicopter?"

"Most suicidal people balk at the last second. They're convinced they want to die, but at the last moment, their lizard brain, the part that is hard-wired to survive at all costs, kicks in and they balk. I hoped the pain of being shot would bring that basic will to survive to his mind before we slammed into a cliff."

"It must've worked. You survived."

I hesitated. "I'm not sure if it was a sudden wish to live, or the bullet hitting the rear rotor controls that caused a controlled crash rather than a total wipe out."

I heard computer keys clicking while I awaited Jack's response. "Reuters has an online report of a Hawaiian helicopter crash that killed the pilot. It says two survivors were transported to the hospital for treatment."

"The two survivors are Jill and me."

"Holy Hannah, there's a video of the firemen hosing down the smoldering remnants of the helicopter. It doesn't appear anyone could've walked away from that wreck."

"We got out immediately after the crash. The fire was really rolling by the time the firemen reached the scene. I assume a lot of the aluminum frame melted in the flames."

"All bullshit aside, how are you and Jill?"

"We're fine."

"Listen, Fletcher. I have to report this incident to my bosses. I need to know the exact extent of your injuries. You'll be investigating polar bear sightings in Denali National Park if you tell me something other than what is later reported by the hospital or media."

Sighing, I said, "I have bruises and second-degree burns on about half my body. There is nothing life-threatening, and my burns will be healed, but still tender, for a week. Jill has a head injury. The doctors are assessing it as we speak. She was lucid, knew what day of the week it was, but thought she'd died and was in hell." I chuckled. "The hell thing was probably due to our crash on a black lava field, the smell of sulfurous vog, and my burned hair."

I heard beeping on the phone and Jack interrupted. "I'll call you back. The DEA is calling."

After disconnecting the call with my boss, I punched in my mother's cell phone number. "Hi Mom. Jill and I will be on the news."

Mother sighed. "Tell me it's because you are so deeply tanned from lying on the beach that the local television station featured you."

"I'm a bit past tan…"

"Don't you know enough to use sunscreen? Overexposure to UV light causes skin cancer."

"Mom…I was in a helicopter crash."

"Oh my God. Is Jill taking care of you?"

"She was beside me in the helicopter. Her head got banged during the crash and the doctors are examining her now."

"I told you to take care of her!"

"Mom, she's as bullheaded as you and Molly are. She volunteered to take a dangerous uncover assignment. We were working for the Drug Enforcement Agency."

"It's time for you to retire. I don't want any more of these calls. Do you understand me?"

"I've got a call on the other line. Goodbye, Mom."

I ended the call to my mother and was laying out my singed clothing when my cell phone rang. The caller ID showed NPSISB. "Hi Jack. What did the DEA say?"

"They thanked us for supporting their Hawaii operation. Overall, they were pleased."

"Overall?"

"The suspect who could've tied all the pieces together was killed in a helicopter crash. The Assistant US Attorney hopes one of the other people they arrested will accept a plea bargain in return for testifying, but the helicopter pilot was their best hope for getting someone high up the chair of command to cop a plea."

"Tell them he was a dead man as soon as he got the call telling him to bug out. He knew the cartel wouldn't let him live to testify, so he was going to crash the helicopter and kill himself."

"You said he'd balk at the last second."

"The DEA doesn't need to know that."

Pardee paused. "Right. There were two surviving witnesses. One of them is telling me the pilot was going to kill himself in a crash. Got it."

"Did the DEA say anything else?"

"The drugs they recovered from the hangar had been transported to Hawaii via sailboat. They're weighing the recovered drugs, but it appears to be the biggest drug bust ever in the Hawaiian Islands. To say they're happy would be an understatement."

"Did they tell you what happened to my confidential informant?"

"They didn't mention a confidential informant."

"Is the Park Service going to get any press out of this?"

"This is the culmination of a multi-year undercover operation. The DEA director made it clear that you and Jill were only involved in the final moments. The official announcement will say that it was an inter-agency operation. I think there will be an asterisk that says, 'including investigators from the National Park Service.'"

I was about to respond to that when a nurse walked in, pointed at the sign forbidding the use of cell phones, then snatched the phone from my hand and ended the call. "You can see your wife now."

"I'll get dressed and be there in a second."

Smiling, the nurse said, "It'll take more than a second for you to get dressed when you feel your clothing sliding over your burned skin. Hold the back of your gown shut and follow me."

Jill's ER room was three doors away from mine. I followed the nurse, dutifully holding the back of my gown so I didn't flash anyone with my bare butt. The lights in Jill's room were subdued, and a different nurse was clearing away what I knew was a suture kit, the supplies used to stitch a wound.

I blanched when I noticed that Jill's head had been shaved above her left eyebrow and there was a lump on her scalp the size of a tennis ball. The raised bruise had turned black, and a neat row of small stitches ran from her hairline upwards and across the lump for about three inches.

Jill looked tired but smiled. "The doctor said she used tiny stitches that won't be visible when my hair grows out." Her smile turned to concern when she saw the white cream on my forearms. "What happened to you?"

"They put goop on some minor burns. I'm fine."

I approached her bed, anticipating a hug, but she held me at arms length. "Your hair is singed, you don't have any eyebrows, and your face is sunburned."

I leaned down and hugged her. "My eyebrows will grow back. How's your head?"

"The nurse said I'd been telling them about my visit to hell."

"Um, yeah. You were dazed. We landed on a black lava field, and you could smell the sulfur in the vog. You were sure we were in hell."

"How did I feel about that?"

"You made a comment about me dragging you down from heaven on my coattails, or something. I told you we'd been in purgatory and had been freed."

"What did I say to that?"

"You wanted to get into a philosophical discussion of Dante's *Inferno*."

Jill looked toward the nurse who'd just disposed of the suture kit. "Never marry a cop. They're all cynical and destined for hell."

"I heard you two helped the DEA bust a big drug ring. I'd think St. Peter would take that into consideration."

Jill looked at the nurse who'd walked me down. "What do you think?"

Shaking her head she replied, "After working in the ER for twenty-two years, I often wonder if there is a God."

"Another victim of reality's cynicism," I replied.

"There's a lot of cynical first responders," the nurse replied. "It's hard to understand how a loving God can allow the terrible things we see."

Our discussion was interrupted when my phone rang. The nurse who was holding it glared at me. "Cell phones aren't allowed in the ER."

I held out my hand. "I'm a federal cop. It might be a call from J. Edgar Hoover."

The nurse handed me the phone. "I think old J. Edgar died a couple decades ago."

Seeing my mother's number on the caller ID I grimaced and handed the phone to Jill. "It's for you."

"Hi, Ronnie. I'm fine. I bumped my head and got a couple stitches, but there's no permanent damage."

The nurse looked at me and mouthed, *Ronnie*?

"Ronald Reagan. He's calling to congratulate us."

Rolling her eyes, the nurse said, "He's dead too." Then the two nurses walked out of the exam room.

After a brief discussion with Jill repeatedly assuring my mother that she was fine and that the incident was not my fault, she disconnected the call. "Your history makes it hard to convince your mother that you're not responsible for anything bad that happens to me."

"I don't know why Mom thinks that."

"She's afraid you'll repeat the mistakes of your first marriage."

"Mom never liked Sherry."

"She loves me and doesn't want you to mess that up."

Shaking my head, I took the phone, then realized I didn't have a pocket. "I spoke with Jack. Aside from me needing to fill out an incident report because I shot the helicopter pilot, we're good. The DEA is going to include us as a footnote in the closure of this case."

Jill swung her legs over the side of the bed, then wobbled. "Oh my. I shouldn't sit up so quickly."

"What do you need? I'll get it for you."

"I have to pee. I need to do that for myself."

I pushed the call button. "I'm sure one of the nice nurses will help you to the bathroom."

* * *

It took a few hours for Jill to be officially released from the ER, but we eventually got dressed and gathered our belongings from the plastic hospital-supplied bags. The nurse walked in with the paperwork, pointing out that Jill had a mandatory follow-up appointment with the neurologist in one week. "How are you getting home?"

My mind ran through the day's events. "We've got a rental car in Waimea and a rental pickup at the Hilo police station."

"Where are you staying?" the smiling nurse asked.

"At a Volcano Village B&B," Jill replied.

"A cab would cost you a fortune. I could call an Uber for you."

The Uber driver was a native islander who provided a running tour guide's description of the areas we passed. As we neared Hilo, I interrupted him. "Drive past the strip club, please."

He glanced at me in the rear-view mirror, then turned the mirror so he could see Jill. Although tired and sore, she nodded.

The club's parking lot was empty, a CLOSED sign hanging on the front door. "It's a little early for them," the driver said. "Do you want to hang around until they open?"

"No, take us to the B&B."

My phone rang as we drove out of Hilo. I almost ignored the blocked number, assuming it was a telemarketer, but answered on the fourth ring. "Yeah."

"Fletcher?" Joe Gray's voice asked.

"Sorry, Joe. I assumed the blocked number was a spam caller."

"We block our outgoing call numbers." He paused. "I heard you guys were injured in the helicopter crash. I just spoke with the ER doctor who reluctantly said you'd been discharged. Citing

HIPAA rules, he refused to provide an update on your condition.”

“Jill’s got a concussion and I’m burned, but we’ll recover.”

“I was asked to relay a message to you. Jocelyn is in protective custody.”

“You’ve got Mocha?”

Gray chuckled. “She’s discarded that moniker and has gone back to her given name.”

“Is she okay?”

“She was rounded up during the bust, but she dropped your name. That information was passed to me, and I pulled her out of the county jail, citing her involvement in federal crimes.”

“Will you be able to protect her?”

“She’s cooperating with us. After the trial, we’ll find a nice place for her to resettle. She mentioned that she’s only a few credits short of getting her teaching degree. I’m sure there will be a school who would be happy to have someone as qualified as Jocelyn as a kindergarten teacher.”

“Thanks for looking out for her. Jill promised to help Mocha.”

“Tell Jill that she’s being well cared for.”

Jill looked at me. “What about Mocha?”

I looked at the driver in the mirror. “Is there a coffee place nearby?”

“Yeah, about a mile ahead there’s a little café. Do you want to stop there?”

I pulled $20 out of my wallet and held it out to him. “Would you get us two black coffees, please?”

“I thought you wanted mocha?”

"I changed my mind."

We sat in the idling Uber while the driver went in to buy coffee for us. "Mocha is in protective custody. They're going to let her finish her teaching degree, then she'll be relocated."

"Where?" Jill asked.

"They wouldn't tell us even if they knew." Seeing Jill's skepticism, I said, "Trust me, it'll be somewhere that her bi-racial heritage and Chicago accent won't stand out."

"I'd like to say goodbye to her."

I shook my head. "She's in protective custody and I'm sure they won't tell us where she is."

"I hope she'll be okay."

I patted Jill's hand. "Mocha has personality and street smarts. She'll be fine."

Chapter 17

The neurologist examined Jill a week later and said she needed to be rechecked in another week. When Jill protested that we were booked on return flights to Texas in three days, the doctor looked at me. "You're cops, right? Do you know what an intracranial hemorrhage is?"

"It's bleeding inside your skull. It's often the cause of death from blunt force trauma to the head," I replied.

"Jill had a minor brain bleed. It isn't dangerous, and it was resolved while she was in the hospital. I don't want it to restart when the plane's cabin pressure drops. Buy her a beach chair and keep her entertained here for another week. Then see me again before you fly."

Jill turned red. "Hey, I'm right here. You don't need to tell my husband what I can and can't do."

The gray-haired doctor turned to her. "Jill, you had a concussion. It might interfere with your judgement for a while. I understand that you're a strong-willed, independent woman, but please lean on your husband for a few more days. Let him drive and make your work and financial decisions."

I smiled at Jill and the doctor. "I guess we should cancel the timeshare presentation."

The doctor looked at me and frowned. "Is being a smartass a job requirement prior to becoming a cop, or do they teach that in the police academy?"

"I came by it naturally," I replied.

The doctor stopped at the door. "Any other questions?"

I smiled. "She's a week past the injury. Would intimate relations be therapeutic?"

I heard the doctor mutter "smartass" as he walked out of the exam room.

Jill slid off the exam table. "Take me to the swimsuit shop."

"You just bought a new swimsuit."

She pointed to her forehead. "I need a sun hat, so I don't burn my scalp while I lounge on the beach."

I held the door open. "After recuperating next to the B&B's pool for the last week, I'd prefer to explore the rest of the island rather than lying on the beach. There's a Kona Coffee Trail where we could visit small coffee roasters and sample their products."

"How much coffee can you drink in a day, Doug?"

"I'm a cop. I'm accustomed to drinking coffee every time the car stops."

Jill slid off the exam table and walked toward the door. "I heard the north shore bluffs are breathtaking."

* * *

We walked out of the clinic to the rental pickup, and I held the door open until Jill was settled inside. "I could become accustomed to your new gentlemanly behavior."

"Bullshit," I replied. I walked around the truck, climbed in, and started the engine. "You heard the doctor. You're a strong-willed, independent woman who's unaccustomed to people opening doors for her and pulling out her chair at the dinner table."

Jill turned to me. The swelling on her head had shrunk, and the dark blue bruising was turning yellow with some of the color drifting toward her left eyebrow. "I give you permission to treat me like a patient for another week. We'll reassess after that."

I drove away from the clinic and turned toward downtown Hilo. "I'll take you back to the bathing suit shop. They had a wide variety of ladies sun hats. After that, we can have sushi."

"Just to be clear. I had a concussion. The blow to my head did *not* result in amnesia that made me forget that I don't eat raw fish."

When my cell phone buzzed, I struggled to get it out of my pocket, handing it to Jill as I turned into a hardware store parking lot. "Jill Fletcher."

"Shit, I thought I'd dialed Doug's number."

Jill looked at the caller ID, then mouthed DEA. "Doug's driving, Joe. I'll put you on speaker."

"Hi guys. There are some developments in the case I thought you'd like to know about."

I frowned, being unaccustomed to other federal agencies willingly offering information I didn't have an urgent need to know. "Sure. What's up?"

"Can you meet me in the Hilo police station in half an hour?" Gray asked.

I looked at Jill, who shrugged. "Jill's just been reassessed at the hospital. We're not available for any helicopter rides."

Gray chuckled. "This doesn't involve undercover work, helicopter rides, or fugitive arrests."

"Does it include coffee?" I asked. "The clinic coffee was terrible."

"I'll make sure we have a pot of genuine Kona coffee in the conference room."

Jill ended the call and held the phone. "What do you think that's about?"

"There's probably a federal shooting review board wanting the details of my firearm discharge inside the helicopter."

"Really? I think that was well justified."

"You know how Jack feels about us firing our weapons."

Jill straightened. "Oh shit. I wonder if some kid found your pistol in the car we left at the heliport and used it in a holdup?"

"If it had been used in a holdup, the local cops or the Bureau of Alcohol Tobacco and Firearms would've called."

There were two marked police vehicles and four civilian vehicles parked in front of the Hilo police station. Jill surveyed the lot. "I don't see a vehicle marked DEA, or a distinctive dark SUV that all the federal law enforcement agencies seem to prefer."

I nodded toward a blue BMW M4. "The DEA prefers vehicles that don't look like cop cars. I'm guessing the sportscar is something seized in a drug bust, then taken over as an official vehicle."

An officer behind a Plexiglass partition looked up as we walked in. "Can I help you?" He asked through a speaker while checking us out. I placed my credentials into a pass-through tray. After glancing at them, the officer nodded and slid them back to me. "You're expected in the conference room.

An electronic door release clicked, and the officer pointed toward the door to our left. "Through the door, then straight ahead."

Joe Gray and Sara McCallie were seated at a table, a coffee carafe and a stack of Styrofoam cups sat on the table. Joe stood when we walked in. "Did you both get a clean bill of health?"

Sara poured coffee as Jill sat. "Not entirely. The neurologist doesn't want Jill to fly for another week. I'm fine."

Sara handed me a cup of coffee as I sat. "You look like a boiled lobster with peeling skin, Doug. I wouldn't say you're fine."

"I'm bruised, but unbroken."

Gray slid a folder to me. "Check out these pictures."

Flipping through them, I nodded. "These prints look like the photos on the memory chip from the broken camera we found on the lava."

"I need you to sign an affidavit stating where you found the camera and what condition it was in when you recovered it."

"Can't you link the ownership to the dead photographer?"

"We've done that, but we need to explain how it came into our custody. We don't want the defense to argue it was seized during an illegal search." He looked at Jill. "And we need an affidavit from you explaining how you recovered the memory card from Steve Langevin's car."

"I assume you want me to clearly state that I was invited to sit in the car, and that the memory card was in plain sight when I removed it."

Gray smiled and turned to the Hilo officer. "I like working with professionals who know the law."

McCallie leaned on the table. "By the way, Langevin's been fired from the police force."

"And arrested?" I asked.

Gray stared at his coffee cup as he slid it in a circle on the table. "His lawyer made an offer that's being considered by the Assistant US Attorney. The lawyer claims that Steve has knowledge of certain evidence that might lead us to bigger fish."

"I'm not sure Langevin is smart enough to string together a cohesive sentence much less lead you to a larger crime ring."

Gray and McCallie glanced at each other. "We're unconvinced too. But he may have enough bullshit to make the Department of Justice offer him a plea deal."

"Is he providing information about the inter-island drug network?" I asked.

"His information relates to…an investigation underway with a different federal agency."

"The young Asian woman at the party," Jill said.

Gray smiled and nodded. "I'm not at liberty to discuss an ongoing investigation involving another agency."

Behind the photos in the folder, I found two affidavits. I signed one and handed the other and a pen to Jill.

She read it. "How did you draft this?"

"We had your earlier comments," McCallie said. "We added the legalese."

Gray smiled. "If things go as planned, Langevin will be relocated and given an assumed name. I suspect a Park Service assignment in Maine might be just the cover he needs for a new life far away from Hawaii."

Jill chuckled. "Acadia National Park is about as far away as you can get from Hawaii."

I shook my head. "Maine is too obvious. I think Acadia has too many visitors, too. What's that obscure park in Nebraska, Jill?"

"Homestead National Monument is like a hundred miles from any interstate highway. The nearest population center is Lincoln, Nebraska, and that's an hour drive." Jill paused. "I had a co-worker who'd been a college party girl. She described her time at Homestead National Monument as an assignment in boredom hell."

Gray chuckled. "Homestead is not a prison, but Steve might prefer prison to that assignment for the rest of his life."

McCallie nodded. "Justice sometimes comes in strange forms."

Gray reached into his black computer bag and handed a square envelope to Jill.

"What's this?" She asked as she ripped open the flap.

"A mutual friend asked me to give it to you."

Jill read the card, then inhaled sharply as tears formed in her eyes. She handed the card to me.

The thank you card was generic, but the signature was unique. *Mocha*

* * *

We packed our bags, bid goodbye to Mary at the B&B, then drove around the southern end of the island. After a stop for fresh banana bread, we drove to an upscale resort in Kailua-Kona. Jill freshened up while I checked out our new location.

Dressed in a Hawaiian shirt and shorts, Jill dried her hair after showering. "What did you find?"

"We're within walking distance of shopping and at least half a dozen restaurants. I think this will be the perfect place to unwind for a couple of days."

"I need to find a hat and sunglasses."

"I'm sure they're available down the block." I took the towel from her and hung it in the bathroom. "Let's take a walk before we go to the luau."

"Luau?"

"The hotel has a luau tonight. I bought tickets."

"I don't know that I'm ready to be seen in public with a half-shaved head and a black eye."

I pulled her to the hotel room door. "No one knows who you are here, and no one cares if part of your head is shaved. People will probably think that you're a late blooming Emo girl."

"You don't have a clue what an Emo girl looks like."

"I get around."

Grabbing my hand, Jill said, "Yeah, right. You're so attuned to pop culture."

In the hotel lobby, Jill stopped in front of a row of shops. "Buy me a wide-brimmed hat, sunscreen, and big sunglasses."

"Okay," I said, not sure of what had catalyzed those comments. I considered our different taste in clothing and accessories. "What are you planning to do?"

"There's a hair salon here and they're going to do something creative with my hair."

"Um, creative?"

Jill pulled me to the front window where a number of women's hairstyles were pictured. "Look at this. The entire left side of this woman's head is shaved, and the other half is back swept. Don't you think I'd look good in this cut?"

Without hesitation I replied. "Yes," while thinking it looked strange on the teenager in the picture. "I doubt they'll be able to squeeze you in right now."

I felt Jill remove my wallet from my back pocket. She opened it and pulled out five $20 bills. "I bet a hundred-dollar tip will motivate one of the stylists to fit me in." Handing me the wallet, she gave me a push. "I'll see you in an hour."

I looked at her skeptically. "Really?"

Her dimples appeared, distracting me from the stitches in her partially shaved scalp and the black eye that was turning green. "I've heard poi is an aphrodisiac,"

A woman walking past overheard that and laughed. "Only if you don't spit it out immediately."

I turned back and kissed Jill. "I love your optimism."

"This will be okay. My hair will grow back. My black eye will fade. Life is good." She looked around to make sure no one was listening. "I hear they serve unlimited mai tais at a luau. You might get lucky tonight."

I kissed her. "I'm lucky every night."

Chapter 18

Matt and Mandy were waiting for us at the Corpus Christi airport luggage carousel. After hugs all around, Matt helped me retrieve our luggage. With our bags beside us, I looked around for Jill and Mandy. "Where are the women?"

Matt chuckled as he wheeled two bags next to me. "Mandy had plans."

We walked to Matt's Park Service pickup. "What sort of plans does Mandy have?"

"Sometimes it's best not to ask." We set the bags in the back of the pickup, then Matt added, "But it's always good to act pleased with whatever happens."

"Got it."

Matt drove to our new house and helped me carry the suitcases to the front door. His smile seemed odd as I unlocked the door. Stepping inside, I was greeted by the smell of flowers, and I was surprised by the lack of cardboard boxes.

"What the hell happened, Matt? The boxes are gone."

"Remember when I told you about not asking but acting pleased."

"Yeah," I replied, setting our luggage in the laundry room.

"Mandy figured that Jill might not feel up to unpacking boxes after her concussion, so *surprise!* The boxes are unpacked, and everything is stowed in a cupboard, closet, or dresser."

"We won't be able to find anything," I protested.

"Trust me. Debutantes know the proper place for everything. If you can't locate something, it's because you'd been keeping it in the wrong place."

I searched Matt's face for any hint that he was kidding, but there was no smile. "Is my underwear in the top drawer of my dresser?"

"I believe that is the proper place for it. So, yes, that's where your underwear is located."

"What's in the second drawer?"

"That would be the proper location for socks and colored t-shirts."

"And the third drawer?"

"The third drawer contains seasonal items, like long-sleeved shirts, sweaters, and such."

"I've never owned a sweater in my life," I said, leading Matt into the kitchen. I opened the cabinet where I would've stored beer mugs and glassware and found spices, arranged alphabetically. "You're shitting me. Who alphabetizes their spices?"

"Mandy."

"Where, in my kitchen, would I find mugs to pour us a couple of beers?"

"That would be in the upper cupboard to the right of the dishwasher. The cabinet directly above the dishwasher contains the dishes and bowls."

I handed Matt two mugs and took beer bottles out of the refrigerator. "Where is the bottle opener?" I asked.

"They're twist-off caps."

"Geez, Matt. Do you have any say in where things are stored?"

He grinned, watching me pour beer into mugs. "Mandy doesn't set foot in the garage except to get into the car. I get to arrange the tools, as long as they look tidy."

We were on the patio drinking our second beer when I heard the front door open. I stood and was about to slide the patio door open when Jill beat me to it.

Her hair had been redone, the shade lighter, and the style involving a swept arrangement that covered the area where the stitches had been. Her makeup was subtle but hid the bruising and made her look a decade younger. She smiled and pushed a pizza box into my hands. "Mandy's getting plates and napkins."

"You look…stunning."

Jill's smile spread until her dimples formed. "We have Mandy to thank for that."

We ate pizza with our fingers, a loophole in the debutante handbook. After slices of key lime pie, Mandy cleared the table and Matt pulled out a laptop computer. He spent a minute connecting cable to the big screen TV he'd mounted on our living room wall while we were in Hawaii.

With the cables connected, he directed us to the couch and chair facing the television. He pulled up something on the computer, and after a couple keystrokes, we were watching the recording of a Hawaiian news broadcast. A reporter was describing the scene of the biggest drug bust in the history of the state. In the background, people wearing DEA t-shirts were loading plastic-wrapped bricks of drugs into the back of a nearly full U-Haul truck. The camera panned to the side of the truck where other agents were counting stacks of one-hundred-dollar bills on a large table.

When the broadcast ended, Matt touched a few computer keys, and logged in to Zoom. The image of a man wearing a US Park Service brown shirt seated behind a desk appeared. "Who's that?" I asked.

Jill shushed me. "That's Arnie Qualls, the director of the Park Service."

Qualls smiled. "Hi Jill. I don't think I've seen you since we worked together in the Ozarks."

"I'm amazed that you remember me. I was Jill Rickowski back then."

"You were a budding professional ranger among a group of seasonal employees. I'm happy to see you again."

"This is Doug, my husband."

"Doug Fletcher, the man who thought shooting the only pilot on a helicopter was a good plan?"

Before I could defend myself, a chime sounded, and Jack Pardee's face appeared in a tiny square next to the image of Jill and me. "Hi folks. It appears the Fletchers made it back to Texas since there's a sand dollar shadow box behind them."

Qualls cut Jack's greeting short. "Superintendent Mattson, thanks for arranging this call with the Fletchers, Jack, and me. I appreciate Jill and Doug taking time at the end of their long travel day to meet with us." Qualls cleared his throat, apparently composing his thoughts. "As you're all aware, National Park Service employees work in relative obscurity, making our parks safe and enjoyable destinations for millions of guests. A ranger's role is intentionally minimalist, assisting visitors, answering questions, and dealing with problems as they arise, remaining in the background while our guests take in the grandeur of the parks. That said, our rangers and volunteers are the fabric that holds the Park Service together.

"This afternoon I sent an email to all National Park Service employees." Qualls read from a piece of paper. "This past week, two of our NPS colleagues volunteered to assist the Drug Enforcement Agency as undercover officers. While attempting to arrest a suspect, NPS Investigators Jill and Doug Fletcher were involved in the kind of circumstances we all dread. The Fletchers kept a drug distributor distracted in a helicopter while his network of suppliers was arrested. During the raids, more than two tons of drugs were seized. While trying to arrest the pilot, the Fletchers were injured when the helicopter they were riding in crashed. Their heroic actions are an inspiration for every US Park Service employee. I've nominated them for the 2023 Harry Yount Award." Qualls set the sheet of paper aside and looked into the camera. "On behalf of myself and the Secretary of the Interior, thank you for your service."

Jill leaned forward. "We appreciate being recognized for our efforts. Thank you, sir."

"Jill, I heard you were injured in the crash. Have you recovered?"

"My stitches have been removed and the doctor gave me a clean bill of health."

"Good. I won't take any more of your time. Enjoy the rest of your evening."

Qualls reached toward the camera then his face disappeared, replaced by an enlarged picture of Jack Pardee. "There's little I can add to the director's comments. Through your actions, we all look good. Thanks."

Pardee disappeared, and Matt shut down the computer. When he looked up, I saw the wetness in his eyes. "Jack Pardee pushed the Yount award nomination up the chain of command. The bosses agreed that your actions reflect well on the National Park Service."

Trying to change the topic I said, "Jack will shit when he sees the swimwear, sun hats, and beach chairs on Jill's expense voucher."

Jill moved across the couch and sat on my lap. "Doug's joking. None of those things are on my voucher, Matt."

"At this point, I think Jack would sign off on a voucher that includes a truckload of hay," Matt quipped, referring to the guide fee Jill had paid in hay bales during an Arizona assignment.

Blowing out a breath, I stated, "I don't like being in the spotlight."

Mandy laughed. "Honey, this doesn't put you in the spotlight. Not even people who work for the Park Service have ever heard of the Yount Award. Your secret is safe."

Jill ran her fingers through my hair. "Our mothers will be pleased."

"My mother will point out that once again, I've put you in the line of fire."

With a southern drawl as sweet as honey Mandy said, "Just set the award plaque in the cupboard. No one will see it."

I glanced at Mandy. "Where does the Yount Award go in the alphabetized spices?"

Without hesitation, Mandy replied, "After wasabi."

"We don't own any wasabi," I replied.

"Doug, that was before I replenished and arranged your spices. Wasabi is a staple for sushi."

Jill lifted my chin, "Yeah, tuna breath. It's a staple for sushi."

"Tuna breath?" Matt asked.

Mandy stood and smiled. "I'll tell you the story on the way home. Pack up your computer gear. I'm sure the lovebirds are exhausted after their travels."

After exchanging hugs with Matt and Mandy at the door, I looked around the kitchen. "Did you know that Mandy was unpacking for us?"

"She was concerned that I wouldn't be able to bend down to empty the boxes after my head injury."

"Jill, she unpacked my underwear and put it in the dresser."

"I know. She suggested that some of your boxers were getting a little threadbare."

"Could you talk with her about boundaries? Even my mother wouldn't put my underwear in a drawer."

Jill pressed herself against me and wrapped her arms behind my head. "She left a present for us in the bedroom."

"Let me guess; it's a room freshener because our bathroom odor didn't meet debutante standards."

Taking my hand, Jill led me toward the bedroom. "Mandy was a bit elusive about it, which makes me think it's something more…personal."

The flat box laying on the bed was wrapped in white tissue paper and tied with a red bow. Jill picked it up and read the card. "It says, 'This is something proper ladies won't admit to owning, but something their husbands can't stop thinking about.'"

"Let me guess. It's a new Glock to replace the one lost in the helicopter fire."

Jill untied the bow, then removed the wrapping paper. She stopped and shook her head. "Uh uh. Nope. Not happening."

"What?" I asked.

"It's a Victoria's Secret box. There is *nothing* they sell that fits my style." She tossed the box to me and crossed her arms. "Go ahead. Open it."

I lifted out a sheer red camisole with matching panties. "Wow."

Jill walked to the bathroom, "Not even in your dreams, cowboy."

"It'll be cooler than your flannel nightgown on these hot Texas nights," I said to the bathroom door.

"I like my flannel nighties."

"Just try these on."

"What's the point? I won't let you see me wearing them. Even if I did put them on, your next move would be removing them."

"Indulge my fantasies."

The door opened a crack and Jill put out her hand. After handing her the box, I stripped to my boxers, turned off the lights, and got in bed. The door opened a crack and the bathroom lights switched off. "Close your eyes."

"The point of them is…"

"Close your eyes."

"Okay. My eyes are closed."

I heard Jill scamper to the bed and felt her jump under the sheets. Anticipating the texture of lace, I was surprised by the flannel I felt on Jill's hip.

"I thought…"

"The box is on a shelf. Someday, if you're very good and I'm very intoxicated, I'll consider modeling it."

"But…"

Jill pressed her hips against me. "You don't need to see me in that outfit. Just the anticipation has provided enough inspiration. Besides, removing the flannel is more challenging."

“You’re a devil.”

“Shh. This is *not* the time for a theological debate.”

The End

Also published by BWL Publishing Inc.

Whistling Pines cozies

Whistling up a Ghost
Whistling Pirates
Whistling Bake Off
Whistling Artist
Whistling Fireman (fall of 2023)

Doug Fletcher mysteries

Stolen Past
Washed Away
Dead in the Water
Death in Shifting Sands
Devils Fall
Prairie Menace
Down River
Burnt Evidence
Gator Bait
Grave Survey
Dead End Trail
The Last Rodeo
Peril in Paradise

Pine County Mysteries

Killer Secrets
Deadly Mixture
Fatal Business
Taxed to Death

Dean Hovey is the award-winning and best-selling author of three mystery series. He uses his scientific background, travel, extensive research, and consultants to add reality and depth to his stories. One reader said his characters are like people he'd like to invite over for a beer and discussion.

Hovey's Fletcher mysteries follow U.S. National Park Service investigators Doug and Jill Fletcher as they solve crimes in a series of parks and national monuments, sometimes with a bit of humor and often with their evolving relationship. The Whistling Pines mysteries are humorous cozies set in a northern Minnesota senior residence, following Peter Rogers, the Whistling Pines recreation director, as he stumbles through the investigation of murders in his small town. The Pine County mystery series follows Sergeant CJ Jensen and Investigator Pam Ryan as they solve murders in rural central Minnesota.

Dean and his wife split their year between northern Minnesota and Arizona.